"Use the ~~stupid picture~~

"Who cares." The bitterness in Cal Buchanon's voice showed that he cared, and cared a great deal.

"I *love* you, Uncle Cal," his niece, Bunny, said, kissing his shadowed cheek. "And you probably saved Miss Avery's job."

Bunny turned and grinned at Tess. "Want me to photograph the other men, too? I'd do a good job. And I'd work cheap—"

"Bunny! You're not going to go around photographing strange men." Cal's eyes, haggard and angry, turned to Tess, drilling into her. She could feel his unvoiced accusation. *This is all your fault.* If he could no longer blame Bunny, then Tess would be the target of his wrath.

She was anxious to flee the whole complicated scene. It reminded her too much of her past.

Bethany Campbell, an English major and textbook consultant, calls her writing world her "hidey-hole," that marvelous place where true love always wins out. Her hobbies include writing poetry and thinking about that little scar on Harrison Ford's chin. She laughingly admits that her husband, who produces videos and writes comedy, approves of the first one only.

Books by Bethany Campbell

HARLEQUIN ROMANCE

HARLEQUIN INTRIGUE

EVERY WOMAN'S DREAM

Bethany Campbell

Harlequin Books

TORONTO • NEW YORK • LONDON
AMSTERDAM • PARIS • SYDNEY • HAMBURG
STOCKHOLM • ATHENS • TOKYO • MILAN

ISBN 0-373-03109-2

Harlequin Romance first edition March 1991

To Jan and Charles C.
and our mutual friend, G.V.,
Nebraska's favorite bachelor

EVERY WOMAN'S DREAM

CHAPTER ONE

A GRAY PIGEON strutted back and forth outside Tess Avery's office window at the Madigan Advertising Agency. From time to time it cocked its head, as if to stare in at Tess at her cluttered desk.

"Ha," the pigeon seemed to say. "Ha. *I'm* free. I can do what I like. I can fly where I want. Ha, ha, ha."

Then fly, Tess thought malevolently. *Go to the sidewalk café and eat crumbs. Go sit on a statue. Go away.*

The pigeon cast her a superior glance and kept waddling along the ledge. Beyond him Tess could see the wide streets and quaint buildings of Omaha's Old Market section. Flower beds bloomed at the intersections and trees nodded in the May breeze. Permanent awnings extended over the boutiques, restaurants and galleries, shading shoppers and tourists from the golden downpour of the strong Nebraska sun.

Normally Tess enjoyed the view. She would look at it and pretend she was in New Orleans or New York's Greenwich Village, someplace far away and glamorous.

Today she enjoyed nothing. She had an evil headache and a deskful of trouble. She had three tasks, which, if not impossible, were improbable and difficult. First, she must find a chimpanzee that could cook and serve a spaghetti dinner. Second, she must find a hundred-year-old man who could tap dance. Third, she must find twelve handsome, single, desirable men. They must all be from the state of Nebraska and must be farmers or ranchers. And they all had to agree to appear on a calendar that would be used to raise money for troubled farmers across the state.

It was the last of these three duties that filled her with resentment. She supposed the calendar was for a good cause, but she disliked the idea behind it. It seemed childish and sexist to her. Besides, she had long ago trained herself to be uninterested in men, handsome or not. Now she would have to go through the indignity of tracking down and capturing twelve of them.

She bit her pencil in frustration and ran her fingers through her curly auburn hair. Someday, she promised herself, she was going to escape to New York and to a job that could be taken seriously. At the Madigan Agency, Tess got all the jobs that were odd, offbeat, or that nobody else wanted. It was far from fulfilling.

Delia, the agency's secretary, entered Tess's tiny office, carrying a box from the French bakery on the corner. She stopped short when she saw Tess with her pencil clenched between her teeth and her head in her hands. Delia, an attractive black woman, was the calm center that held the ad agency together through its never-ending crises, large and small.

Delia raised an eyebrow skeptically. "Wait. You're tearing your hair. You're eating your pencil. You're giving the pigeon dirty looks. Let me guess. You're not happy?"

"Right," Tess said around the pencil.

Delia gave a philosophical shrug. "You got the dirty job again. Because you're the newest member on the staff. Madigan handed out new assignments this morning, didn't she?"

Tess nodded. "I have to take over the Pasquerali Restaurant television commercials. I have to find a chimpanzee who can make spaghetti."

"Uh-oh," said Delia. "That means the Monkey Man. Good luck."

Tess nodded again and sat back in her swivel chair. Not only did she have to do all these ridiculous jobs, she had to do them well. Her future was at stake. If she did well this spring, Mrs. Madigan had promised to recommend her for a job in New York.

New York, Tess thought, with a pang of yearning. New York—the center of opportunity, power, glamour, talent, style, excitement, creativity. The heart of the advertising world, the home of the finest ad agencies in the country. The place she'd dreamed of for years. There she might do work that was significant. She didn't want to spend her life advertising breakfast sausages and cocktail lounges. She was interested in more important causes: public service campaigns promoting education, health and worthwhile charities.

But standing between Tess and New York was a trio of obstacles. The first was the Monkey Man. If anybody in the Midwest wanted a trained animal, he contacted him, Thurmond Spreckles. There was little choice.

Any animal hired from Thurmond was well behaved and perfectly disciplined. Unfortunately, the same could not be said for Thurmond. If his animals acted like humans, he, in turn, acted like an animal, at least where women were concerned. Tess, who had perfected the art of being cool toward men, intrigued Thurmond and brought out his worst.

Delia patted Tess's shoulder. "Don't take it so hard. You can always wear armor."

Tess shook her head and contemplated the bite marks on her pencil. "Do you know what it's like to be pinched by that man?" She shuddered.

"Girl, we all know what it's like to be pinched by that man. Cheer up. This, too, shall pass away."

"Not only will I have to dodge Thurmond Spreckles, I've got to find a hundred-year-old man who can tap dance."

Delia whistled. "The talent agency's going to love you when they hear that. What for, may I ask? Here, have some calories. You need serious sugar therapy."

Tess took the last pastry in the box, a Napoleon bar, and set it on her desk. Her appetite had vanished during the morning's staff meeting.

"Mercer's Music Store wants a series of TV spots to celebrate its hundredth anniversary. Leon Mercer came up with the bright idea of an elderly man tap dancing up a storm. Then we'll voice-over the slogan, 'Mercer's—after a hundred years—still the liveliest thing on the music scene.'"

"Hmm," Delia said. "Are you going to eat that Napoleon bar or just stare sadly at it?"

"Stare. Do you want it?"

"Yes. I've been dieting since seven o'clock this morning, and it's killing me. If you give it to me, I'll listen to the rest of your problems. I'll even be sympathetic."

Tess made a gesture of futility. "Help yourself. I'll do anything for sympathy. I also got the Homestead Heritage calendar project."

Delia took the Napoleon bar and sat down across from Tess. "Ah," she said happily, "sustenance. What's wrong with that? Homestead Heritage is a good cause, right? Sounds like the kind of thing you've always wanted to do. What's the calendar project?"

Tess watched Delia attack the pastry and felt envious. Her own stomach was full of knots. "It's Mrs. Madigan's pet. We're doing it for charity. To raise money to help farmers in financial trouble."

Delia licked a drop of cream filling from her forefinger. "How public spirited of Mrs. Madigan. And how unusual. What's she care about farmers?"

Tess threw down her pencil and began toying with a stack of video cassettes. "She was raised on a farm. She's sentimental about farms. So she volunteered *me* to help."

"You, I take it, are not sentimental about farms?"

Tess bit the corner of her lip. She was a slender young woman of medium height. She had short russet hair and large dark eyes that could flash or dance with the quick tides of her emotions. But she had long ago learned to suppress emotion when she had to. Mention of the past made her guarded.

"I'm most *definitely* not sentimental about farms. Small farmers can't survive these days. Everybody knows it. Selling some silly calendar won't help."

"Well, if Mrs. Madigan wants it done, it's got to be done. What do you do? Send a photographer out to take pictures of the waving wheat and the lonely windmills and the contented cows?"

Tess threw her a rueful glance. "I should be so lucky. Somebody at the Homestead Heritage Foundation decided we needed a calendar that would really *sell*. They want men on it, bachelors. A North Dakota Farm Help project did the same thing and got a lot of publicity. I've got to find twelve men who ranch or farm, are single, gorgeous and willing to pose—for free."

Delia almost choked on the last bite of the Napolean bar. She seized a napkin and brushed the crumbs from her red skirt. She laughed. "You get to find twelve handsome single men? And you complain? Honey, most women dream of a job like that. Heck, I'd like to find *one* handsome single man. He wouldn't even have to be all that handsome."

Tess stood and stared pensively out the window. The pigeon stared back. *Ha, ha, you're caught in a box,* the pigeon seemed to say. *I can come and go as I please. Ha, ha, ha.* Then it spread its wings and flew away to the east, toward the river.

Tess turned to Delia again. She straightened the jacket of her navy-blue suit. "Delia," she said firmly, "you promised to be sympathetic."

Delia grinned. "I sympathize about the chimp. I sympathize about the tap dancer. But being told to find twelve handsome bachelors—? Like I say, honey, it's every woman's dream."

Tess paced the three steps that it took to cross her office. "I'm not interested in bachelors, handsome or otherwise."

Delia's smile faded. She gave Tess a wry look. "I've been meaning to have a talk with you about that. A nice bachelor could add quality time to your life. All you do, girl, is work, work, work."

Tess paced back three paces. She jiggled her chunky beaded necklace. "I like to work, work, work. I don't have time to get involved with a man. I have a career to build. I don't want to spend the rest of my life in Omaha, doing small-time commercials with chimpanzees—or chasing men for some silly calendar."

Delia made an impatient face. "You still got that bug in your head about going to New York?"

Tess's normally animated face once more went carefully blank. "Yes. I'm twenty-six. It's time to make my move."

Delia shook her head so that her gold earrings swung. "You haven't ever been to New York. You might not like it. It's all scrunched together. It's not friendly, like here. It's not for everybody. I spent six months there. Then I came *home*. I like some space around me. I like to see the sky. I like to walk through the park in broad daylight and not worry about somebody hitting me upside the head. This is a good place."

Tess stared down at the street. Next to one of the circular flower beds along the street stood a bay horse, basking in the sunshine. It was hitched to an ornate white carriage. Its driver sat in the shade of a plum tree, sipping coffee while he waited for passengers. The scene looked like one from another century, a slower, more picturesque one.

"It's a good place," Delia repeated. "It's a wonderful city. It's a *homey* city. It's a homey *state*."

Tess shook her head. "Not to me. Too many memories. I want to move on."

Delia looked at her and sighed. "Honey, it isn't Nebraska you want to leave. It's your past. And I got bad news. When you go, it goes right along with you. It's like your shadow. It's yours, and it sticks with you."

Tess said nothing. If pasts were indeed like shadows, her own felt particularly long and dark. She didn't like to look back. The memories were troubling.

Her adolescence in the straight-laced little town of Cottonwood, Nebraska, had been scarred by strife. She could remember no happiness in the house after her mother's death.

Tess's mother had died when Tess was twelve. Her parents had still been trying to hang on to the farm, and to supplement the budget her mother had taken a job in town as a legal secretary. One snowy morning on her way to work, her car went into a skid and hit an empty cattle truck returning from Omaha.

Lana Avery survived for almost a week in the hospital. Physically she was alive because machines kept her so, but her quick, loving mind had sunk into nothingness, blown out like a candle. Tess's father stayed by her side a long time. At last he told the doctors to shut off the life-support machines.

Sometimes Tess thought her father died that day, as well as her mother. He was never again the same man. A harsh stranger took his place. He sold the farm and took the children to town, where he bought a service station. All he thought of was work. Never an easy going man, he became increasingly strict and severe, especially with Tess.

Tess's two older brothers already were close-mouthed, self-contained young men who took life as it came and asked no questions. They adjusted to the change in their father without comment. Tess could not.

The more she fought her father's rules and strictures, the more unbending he grew. She had once loved Frontier County. She grew to hate and resent it.

Even more she grew to hate her father's increasing narrow-mindedness. "Act like a woman," he'd say whenever she asserted any independence or spoke her mind. "The man is the boss," he'd say. "Remember your place." Her brothers acted as if this outlook was perfectly natural. They were men, they were important, they kept the family business running. She was only Tess, the girl.

In school, however, she did well; far better than her brothers had. In school she felt like somebody almost important. Her father seemed to sense this and dislike it. "Don't get big ideas," he would say when she showed him her report card. "Grades don't mean anything. They don't count for anything in real life."

When she graduated from high school, she was awarded a scholarship in business to attend the University of Nebraska at Omaha. Her father said she couldn't take it, that women had no place in the business world. There was no sense, he said, wasting her time and his money on a college education when in the end all she would do was get married.

They quarreled horribly, until at last he told her she could either obey his wishes or leave his house.

She left. She had her graduation money and the money she'd made throughout high school from selling her 4-H calves: five hundred and twelve dollars. She took the bus to Omaha, rented a room and got a job as a waitress.

She put herself through college by sheer determination—she could be as single-minded and stubborn as her father when she chose. She lost herself in her studies. She paid no attention to men, feeling she'd taken enough orders from them to last her a lifetime. It took her five long years but she graduated from the university with a master's degree in marketing and a straight-A average.

She passed up her first career choice, teaching, because it paid poorly. She chose advertising instead. She intended to make enough money to be free and independent for the rest of her life.

Tess communicated with her father and brothers but only enough to remain on polite terms. They, in turn, made little effort to keep in touch with her. It was, she thought, as if she'd never belonged among them, never had a family at all.

These days she poured all her energy into her job. But she found even work wasn't enough to use all of her ferocious energy. Something seemed missing from her life. There was an emptiness that haunted her and made her feel that even now, after all of her efforts to escape, she was still trapped.

There was a big world out there with big prizes to win, she told herself. There was nothing to hold her in Nebraska. All it offered her, she told herself, was memories of hard work and sacrifice. She was filled with the urge to break with the past completely, go to New York and fill the void in her life. She would find more challenging horizons, more meaningful work. That was her only ambition now, and it consumed her.

The silence in the small office grew awkward. Delia stood. She put one hand on her hip. "Look, Tess, I'm sorry I brought up the past. I know you don't like to talk about it. But it's the one piece of baggage you never lose, no matter how far you travel. I just want the best for you."

Tess gave her a shaky smile. Delia was the only person in Omaha she had ever told about her family. "It's all right. It's just that these idiotic assignments have me down."

"Hey," Delia said, smiling again. "You'll do fine. Remember last month? When you had to do the commercial with the chickens dressed like chorus girls? And you thought you'd go crazy trying to keep the high heels on their little chicken feet?''

Tess smiled, too.

"You're probably the only woman in Nebraska who ever taped dancing shoes on a bunch of hens."

Their eyes met as a spark of understanding flashed between them. They both laughed at the absurdity of what they went through to earn a living.

"I've got to get back to work," Delia said, "or Mrs. Madigan will pounce on me and deliver the efficiency lecture. Good luck with the chimp and the tap dancer. And with those twelve handsome bachelors—you poor thing. Lunch at the sidewalk café?"

Tess nodded, and then Delia was gone, with a swirl of her red skirt and a jingle of her long gold earrings. She left behind the scent of her carnation perfume, clean and spicy.

Tess sat down at her desk again. She picked up the phone and dialed the number of Thurmond Spreckles, who billed himself as the Monkey Man. In her most businesslike tones, she told him what she wanted.

"Pasquerali's wants to show the chimp cooking and serving spaghetti and making a mess. Then they want to show how elegantly it's done at their restaurants. Their slogan is 'Pasquerali's—we don't monkey around.' "

"I can teach Pooky to make spaghetti," Thurmond Spreckles said. "I can even teach her to make good spaghetti. I can have her trained so you can get your footage in one working day, guaranteed. It'll cost you fifteen hundred bucks, plus expenses."

Tess gritted her teeth. Trained chimpanzees didn't come cheaply. "Fine. I'll want her June fifth—in three weeks."

"And your body. I want your body, too," Thurmond said, lechery resonating in his voice. Tess saw him in her mind's eye, and the picture repulsed her. He was a pale, skinny man with long red hair worn in a ponytail. He always smelled like whatever animal he had been working with most recently.

"Don't even think about it. Bring the chimp and leave your libido at home. I *mean* it."

"I mean it, too. I want your body, your body, your body," said Thurmond, pretending to breathe hard. "I want to melt that wall of ice around you. I want—"

Tess hung up. For a moment she put her head in her hands again. Then she took a deep breath and dialed Talent Scouts, the city's biggest talent agency.

"I need a hundred-year-old man who can tap dance," she told Jerry Birch. "I need him a week from Thursday."

"Ha, ha," said Jerry. "You're kidding."

"Jerry, I'm not kidding. Leon Mercer wants a tap dancer for his anniversary spot, and he insists the guy actually be a hundred years old. Or at least close."

"Tess," Jerry's voice was flat with weariness, "why is it always *you* who calls up and asks me for something impossible?"

"To keep you on your toes. A hundred-year-old tap dancer, Jerry. A week from Thursday. Can you find him for me?"

"Aaargh," said Jerry. "Why wasn't I a priest, like my mother wanted? Okay, I'll do my best. Tell Leon Mercer I hate him, will you?"

"Sorry," Tess said with false cheer. "The customer is always right. We live to serve, you and I."

She hung up, praying that Jerry would come through for her. Then she turned to her typing table and started to draft the ad that would run in every paper in the state:

Wanted: volunteers. Male models needed for Homestead Heritage fund-raising calendar. Must be farmers or ranchers, single, between ages eighteen to forty-five. Color photographs, preferably .35 mm, and biographical information. Send to Calendar Project, Madigan Advertising Agency, Old Market Mall, Suite D, Omaha. This is a charitable project—no payment involved.

Tess's mouth crooked sardonically. She wondered how much nut mail the ad would generate. Loads of it, if she guessed right. She ran her hand through her tousled russet curls.

In her imagination she could already hear cameras starting to click, click, click, all across the state.

CLICK, CLICK, CLICK. It's not so much what you're shooting or who, but how you do it, thought Bunny Sevrinson. It's your eye. It's how you see light and shadow, color and shape. It's your inner vision, that's what. *Click, click, click.*

Bunny was seventeen years old, and she was hiding in the lilac bushes at the edge of the pasture. She'd read the ad for male models in the *Lawler County Trumpet*, and she was determined to come up with a winner. And while Bunny knew it was creativity and inner vision that counted most in a photograph, she knew that it didn't hurt to have a model who was a hunk.

Her Uncle Cal was a royal pain, always trying to run her life, but he nevertheless qualified as a hunk. At least all her friends thought so, and giggled and screamed and acted like idiots whenever they talked about him. But they didn't have to live with him and be bossed around by him all the time. Outwardly a hunk, inwardly a tyrant, Bunny thought, training her telephoto lens on him again. A tyrant she planned to leave behind as soon as possible, one way or another. In the meantime, she might as well exploit the fact he was a hunk.

This was going to be a great set of shots, Bunny thought, squaring her jaw. One of the hired hands had reported that the little palomino colt in the near pasture had a hurt leg. She'd overheard and seen Cal, who'd been splitting fence posts, leave for the pasture. She'd snatched up her camera and headed for the shelter of the lilac bushes, a determined glint in her eye.

The light was great, Bunny thought, bringing her uncle into sharper focus. It was late afternoon, when the slanting rays of the sun made long shadows in the grass, and the air seemed filled with flecks of gold.

As for her uncle, she grudgingly admitted, he really wasn't bad for an old guy of thirty-seven. He was bare chested and wearing low-slung faded jeans and black cowboy boots. He had broad shoulders, hardly any hips, and thigh muscles that rippled with each step he took. The early-summer sunshine had already burnished him to the color of copper.

His hair was black, slightly too long to be fashionable, and it fell in an unruly wave over his forehead. He had intense hazel eyes under dark brows, a straight nose and a rather wide mouth with an upper lip that took some interesting curves. No, Bunny thought, not bad at all for an older guy who was also a world-class killjoy.

Click, click, click.

He had the little palomino colt in his arms, and it nuzzled his bare shoulder. Sometimes it would look up, as if curious, at Cal's unsmiling face. That, Bunny thought, was a great shot. *Click, click.*

The colt's long golden legs dangled, and its mane and tail looked snowy white against Cal's suntanned chest. He was only ten or so yards away from Bunny now. She retreated farther into the lilac bushes and kept snapping away. He seemed to be heading straight for her—terrific luck. He must be going to go through the fence instead of using the gate, so he'd be closer to the stable.

She fiddled expertly with her lenses and focused on him again. He was close enough now that she could see the veins standing out in his arms and the way shadows played under his moving muscles. He shifted the colt slightly and once again it turned its dark eyes up to him. There was a long, low cloud behind them, and the setting sun had turned it as gold as the little palomino's coat. It made Cal's skin seem more bronze, his hair darker, his hazel eyes more intense.

Great stuff, thought Bunny, I am a *genius*. Wait until Fred sees this. Fred was the older man, very bright and artistic, who was interested in her. Fred was almost a soul mate. Unlike her uncle, he had great faith in her talent.

Her uncle walked almost right past her. He paused. He didn't even glance at the lilacs.

"Bunny, get out of the bushes," he said out of the side of his mouth. "And stop taking pictures of me. I don't like it."

Her heart almost stopped beating. She stayed motionless in the lilacs. He couldn't have seen her. She must have imagined he'd said that.

"Bunny!" His tone was so edged, so dangerous, that she jumped in spite of herself. "Go do your homework. Now. Or I confiscate every roll of film you own."

He'd do it, too, the dictator, Bunny thought, narrowing her eyes. Reluctantly she stepped from the cover of the lilac bushes.

"I mean it." Cal's face was grim. "Go do your math."

Bunny tossed her long blond hair and said nothing. He wouldn't be bossing her around much longer. In a week she'd graduate from high school. She would work all this summer in the photography studio in the neighboring town, and then, although Cal didn't know it, she intended to escape. Escape the farm, escape Nebraska, and especially escape her uncle. She and Fred just hadn't decided precisely how.

She patted her camera protectively. Cal was actually going to help her make her getaway, but he didn't know that, either.

She fell in step beside him. She glanced up at his implacable expression.

He threw her a brief but withering look. "Why're you out here? You're supposed to be studying for your finals."

Bunny shrugged nonchalantly. She was a tall girl, but looked almost small beside Cal, who was six foot four in his boots. She had his deep-set hazel eyes and straight nose, and she had the same stubborn mouth as he did. Slim as a reed, she gave off a deceptive impression of fragility.

"I was just shooting because the light was interesting," Bunny lied. "Fred said I should practice unposed shots. That's all."

He gave her another of his I'm-the-lord-and-master-of-this-household looks. He didn't approve of Fred and had made it clear in no uncertain terms.

Bunny looked as innocent as possible. Cal wouldn't be her lord and master much longer. He was a spoilsport, a killjoy and a wet blanket, and she intended to leave him far, far behind.

But at least he was good-looking, and that she could use to her very great advantage. She looked up at his profile and patted her camera again.

Would she ever use him. She'd show him. Would she ever.

TESS HAD RUN the ad for models in papers across the state. By the Monday after its first appearance, she'd had two replies. The next day there were seven more. On Wednesday, another eighteen arrived. On Thursday morning, the mailman dropped fifty-two envelopes on Delia's desk. Fifty-one were addressed to the Calendar Project. One was addressed to Tess. It was a note from Thurmond Spreckles, the Monkey Man, and contained an indecent proposition.

Tess read the note, blushed and threw it in the wastebasket. This morning she had to go with the video production crew to shoot the tap-dancing commercial. She didn't want to face the rest of her mail, not yet. The photos that had come in so far for the calendar project were not promising. Only one real candidate had emerged, a rancher from Cherry County. He was a nice-looking man, but about fifteen pounds overweight. Tess thought they had no choice but to use him.

"I can't take any more would-be calendar boys," Tess told Delia. "I've got to go watch the hundred-year-old man and pray we don't dance him into his grave. *You* can go through the goodies today."

"Right on," said Delia. "It's a dirty job, but somebody has to do it." She opened the first envelope and drew out a picture. She squinted at it for a long moment in distaste. "Yuk. This man isn't good-looking. He hardly has any chin. And he's got ears like jug handles."

"Sounds like he might be one of the winners," Tess said, shaking her head. "This state is famous for good-looking men. Where are they hiding?"

She slung her purse over her shoulder, tucked her briefcase under her arm and left Delia opening another envelope. As she closed the door, she heard Delia say, "Oh, *really*. Yuk!"

Tess returned, three hours later, exhausted from worrying about the hundred-year-old man. He had actually been only ninety-three, remarkably spry, and far more enthusiastic about the project than Tess. She could still picture him decked out with a candy-striped jacket, white straw hat, and a cane which he expertly twirled. An old vaudevillian, he'd said he loved performing again, and kept insisting on doing more takes. He'd constantly thought of new twists to throw into his number. Tess had been certain he would dance himself to death's door, but he left the session in far better shape than she did. She felt wrung out as a rag.

Now she blew a curl out of her eyes and sat down in front of Delia's desk. She put her hands to her temples and rubbed.

"You look like you're the one who tap-danced all morning," Delia said. "Everything go all right?"

"The man was wonderful. Fantastic. He'll charm everybody. We'll probably win an award for this. But it took five years off my life, I swear. I have no energy left. None."

Delia, who looked stunning today in a pink shirtdress, gave her a cryptic smile. "I can recharge your batteries."

Tess sat up straighter and smoothed out the skirt of her green knit suit. "Nobody can recharge my batteries. I have five radio spots to write by next Monday. Plus, next week I have to work all day with Monkey Man. Eight full hours. I can't face it."

"Oh, I think I can put all that out of your mind." Delia kept her mysterious smile as she picked up a large yellow envelope. She pretended to fan herself with it.

"Don't tell me you found something worthwhile in all those pictures. That's too much to hope for."

Delia made a wry face. "Oh, I found lots. I found some seriously un-goodlooking men. I found a couple who are definitely strange. They sent pictures of themselves with no clothes on."

Tess squeezed her eyes shut, ran her fingers through her hair and shook her head to clear it. "I knew it. I knew it. An ad like that makes the weirdos crawl out of the woodwork. It happens every time."

"But," Delia continued, still fanning herself with the envelope, "I found a couple of definite possibilities. A college boy out in Cheyenne County. A sugar beet farmer from Buffalo County, about forty. And—" she paused for emphasis "—I found this. Rejoice. Somebody up there likes you."

Tess took the envelope. She opened it. It contained not one picture, but a small stack. She looked at the top one.

A dark-haired man stared back at her from the photo. He was bare-chested. His hair fell over his forehead, and his eyes were beautiful. He held a gangling little palomino foal in his arms, and the animal gazed up at him with what seemed both curiosity and trust. Behind the man's broad-shouldered figure, the sky was streaked with gold.

"Good grief," Tess said, her mouth falling open slightly. "Is he *real*?"

"He's real—he raises cattle and horses up in Lawler County, he's thirty-seven years old, owns his own ranch, and he's single."

Tess kept staring at the dark-haired man, transfixed. He was the perfect model, an advertiser's dream. He almost made her forget for a moment that she wasn't interested in men. "He's too good to be true."

She fanned through the pictures. They were all variations of the same scene, the bare-chested man holding the foal, the wide Nebraska sky behind him.

"His name is Cal Buchanon," Delia said. "There's only one catch."

Tess couldn't look away from the pictures. Her hands almost shook with excitement. "Of course. There's always a catch."

"The photographer's his niece. Buchanon says we have to use one of her shots. If these aren't suitable, she'll take more. And he's already signed releases for us to use these."

Tess shook her head in disbelief. "That's no problem. These photos are great. They could be professional. He's signed releases for them? We have permission to use them? They're *ours*?"

Delia patted a sheaf of papers in affirmation. "Signed, sealed and delivered. What do you think?"

Tess swallowed and licked her lips. She looked up from the pictures and into Delia's dancing eyes. "I think we just got lucky. This man could sell a million calendars."

"That's what Mrs. Madigan says. She wants you to send this guy's photo to all the papers for advance publicity. You know, spark interest in the project. And she wants you to write the press release to go with it. Even send it to some of the national women's magazines—we'll have women from all over the country waiting for this calendar. The North Dakota calendar got national coverage. We will, too. We'll use this guy as the teaser—you know—make him sound like every woman's dream."

Tess nodded numbly. Her eyes, trained once more on the handsome man's face, grew troubled.

Everything *did* seem too good to be true. She reminded herself that the man was little more than a glorified farmer, and that if he wasn't married, something was probably seriously wrong with him. He was probably mean or stupid or conceited or strange. But he didn't look mean or stupid or conceited or strange. He looked dependable and intelligent, albeit a bit brooding.

And he'd already signed the releases. The pictures belonged to the Homestead Heritage project to use for the calendar.

"There's something peculiar about this," Tess muttered. "Let me see those releases. You said a letter came with them?"

Delia handed her the releases and a typewritten letter. It gave a brief biography of Buchanon. He had master's degrees in business and agriculture from the University of Nebraska. At the age of twenty-four he had taken over the family ranch. He had also helped raise his deceased sister's three children. The myriad responsibilities had kept him too busy to marry.

The youngest of the children, Barbara Jean, had taken the pictures, and Buchanon would consent to be part of the calendar project only if one of her photographs of him was used. In the meantime, he would be out of the state for the next month. Any correspondence should be sent to the niece in care of Lawler, Nebraska, post office box. No phone calls, please.

Everything was signed with the same signature, Cal Buchanon, in a bold black flourish.

All the signatures looked perfectly legitimate and unquestionably masculine.

They should have. Bunny had worked diligently to forge them. And her uncle had no idea of what she'd done.

Not yet, he didn't.

CHAPTER TWO

POOKY THE CHIMPANZEE spent the morning making spaghetti. The script called for her to make it as untidily as possible. Pooky, who always threw herself into her parts, very nearly threw herself into the cooking kettle as well. Tomato sauce spattered everywhere. Oregano was hurled like confetti. Meatballs were tossed with enthusiasm and resounding splats.

"Great work, Pooky." Tess gave the chimp an affectionate tickle under the chin. She straightened the ape's stained chef's hat. "You're a wonderful girl, Pooky. Everybody's going to love you."

The chimp looked up at her with its sad, all-too-human eyes. Then it gave her a broad smile, pushed up Tess's skirt and kissed her wetly on the kneecap.

Tess jumped, for at the same moment, a pair of lanky arms went around her waist from behind. A pointed chin rested on her shoulder. "I taught her that. It's what I want to do myself. Kiss your beautiful dimpled knees. Can I?"

It was, of course, the Monkey Man, Thurmond Spreckles, and he was squeezing the breath out of her. He smelled like chimpanzee and unwashed laundry. He dug his sharp chin deeper into her shoulder. He tried to nibble her ear.

"Please!" Tess elbowed free from his unwanted embrace. She brushed off the sleeves of her white blouse. He'd gotten oregano and chimpanzee hair on her.

"Will I please kiss your knees? You bet." He moved, as if trying to maneuver her into a corner.

"No," retorted Tess, her dark eyes blazing, "please don't make me kill you. I respect you as an animal trainer. As a person, however, I find you—" She paused. She wanted to say *repulsive*, but she had, after all, to work with him. "I find you're—not my type. Please don't touch me again. My nerves are on edge, and I might overreact. And if I overreact, you'll regret it."

He didn't back off. "Sticks and stones may break my bones, but whips and chains excite me—"

"Thurmond!" Tess warned, truly angry. "You're a sick person. Do you know that?"

"I love it when you say my name," he said, inching closer. "Want to go out to my van?"

"Thurmond!" Tess clenched her fists.

Pooky, sensing tension, began to jump about nervously. "Oook, oook, oook!" she cried. She knocked over a light stand.

"Oh *hell*," said Thurmond, backing off. "Pooky, stay away from the lights."

Tess sighed with relief and adjusted her white, pleated skirt. She still felt the chimpanzee kiss tingling on her knee.

"Miss Avery?" Lorne, the chief cameraman, said, "you've got a call in the other room. Look, you want me to help keep that guy away from you?" He nodded at Thurmond, who was scolding Pooky so unmercifully that the animal was cowering under a table, trying to hide.

"No thanks, Lorne. I can handle him. Another four hours and it's over." *Four hours*, she thought, feeling more dejected than Pooky.

She went to the front room. They were using the kitchen of one of the crewmen to shoot the cooking scene with Pooky.

It was a relief to get away from the makeshift set, away from Thurmond and his everlasting propositions. How did his animals turn out so sweet, she wondered in frustration, when he was so horrid? She picked up the phone.

"Hello?"

"Tess—it's me, Delia. How's the shoot going?"

"The ape is delightful. The man is deplorable. The spaghetti's everywhere. If you called to give me bad news, don't. Have mercy."

A pause hung in the air, just long enough to be sinister. "I don't have time to be merciful," Delia said. "We have a problem. We have to move quickly. It's the calendar project."

Tess wrinkled her brow. "What's wrong? We've picked fifteen potential candidates. We've got a decent lineup, very respectable. We've already got a release from the best one— the Buchanon man. Did you see the story in the *World-Herald* last night? With his picture? Three different women in my neighborhood told me he was the best-looking man they'd ever seen."

Tess heard Delia swallow. "Yes. Well. Women have called here, too. The man's created a sensation. But we've hit a snag."

"How?" Tess felt her head starting to pound. She began rubbing her temple. It was something she did often lately. "What could go wrong, Delia? We've got the pictures. He signed the releases."

"No." Delia's voice was strained in its effort to sound calm. "He didn't sign the releases. He never saw the pictures. He never sent them. He never wrote the letter."

"What?" Tess shut her eyes in pained disbelief. Her head throbbed harder. *"What?"*

Delia sounded depressed and disgusted. "The letter was a phony. His signature was forged on everything. Tess, he's furious. He's talking about a lawsuit over the press releases. And he says there's no way he'll be in the calendar. None."

"A lawsuit?" Tess was horrified. "Not be in the calendar? He's *got* to. He's our strongest selling point. Mrs. Madigan insists on him. Good grief, Delia, I've even sent that press release to national publications—and his picture. We've got to make him listen to reason."

"Honey, this man is so angry, he's not going to listen to *anything*. He's one tough customer."

Tess felt slightly sick. A lawsuit. And an angry, tough customer, determined to torpedo her project. "I'll call him."

"He's unplugged his phone. The last thing he said before he hung up was not to bother him. He said we could talk to his lawyer, Noble J. Jennings."

Tess gritted her teeth. "Does Mrs. Madigan know?"

"She's the one he called. He read her the riot act. She actually looked scared."

Tess rubbed her temple harder. Mrs. Madigan—scared? Tess had never seen her look even slightly alarmed. The woman had nerves of cast iron. "What does she think we should do?"

"She wants you to drive up and talk to him in person."

"Talk to him? This is a man so ferocious he's got Mrs. Madigan scared, and she wants *me* to talk to him?"

"Yes. Tonight."

"Tonight?" Tess almost wailed. "Delia, do you know what I've gone through today? I've spent all morning with a chimpanzee throwing meatballs and Thurmond Spreckles trying to lift up my skirt. I can't drive clear up to Lawler County—not tonight—"

"Honey, you've *got* to. Mrs. Madigan's very upset about this. She wants this man. She thinks the success of the calendar depends on him. This project is her baby."

And I'm the baby-sitter, thought Tess, feeling queasier than before. *If I don't save it for her, she won't recommend me for the job in New York. She might even fire me. My brilliant career's over before it's started.*

She was silent a long moment. She twirled a strand of hair so hard that it hurt. What kind of man was Cal Buchanon? How could he be such a poor sport? Why couldn't he contribute one measly photograph to a charitable project? His stubbornness was posing a personal threat to her, to both her job and her future. She didn't like threatening men. They reminded her of her father, all temper and stubbornness and do-it-my-way-or-else.

"Well," she said fatalistically, "I guess I drive to Lawler County. I'll probably never return. My car, you know is a scrap heap. I'll be lucky to make it to the city limits."

"I know. Sorry, Tess. But who expected this?"

Tess shook her head and sighed. "The niece must have done it, didn't she? She wanted her pictures used."

"I suppose." Delia sighed, too. "I'd like to get my hands on her, the sneak."

"She may help us, actually," Tess reasoned, desperate for any scrap of hope. "I mean, we acted in good faith. She must have been the one to falsify everything, wanting a photo credit. When he cools down, he'll have to see that. Won't he? We're both innocent parties—he and the agency."

"You can hope. Mrs. Madigan said talking to him was like talking to a barbed wire fence. He was cutting, and he didn't give an inch."

"I'll do what I can."

She told Delia goodbye and hung up the phone. She turned and gazed out the window a moment. She rubbed her temples again.

She didn't hear Thurmond moving up behind her. She suddenly sensed his unwashed smell and felt his moist and bristly kiss making a wet *smack* against the back of her neck.

She whirled and found herself practically in Thurmond Spreckles's arms. "Your neck," he said, breathing hard. "It's irresistible." He tried to embrace her, leaning toward her as if to kiss her.

She dodged and pushed him away, accidentally stepping on his foot with her three inch heel. She thought she heard a slight crunch, perhaps of a toe bone.

"Ouch!" Thurmond jumped backward and sat on the sofa, snatching up his wounded foot. It was encased in a dirty jogging shoe. "You almost *impaled* me," he accused. "You did that on purpose, Avery!"

"No," Tess said between her teeth. "But I wish I had. And next time I will, I *swear* it." She stalked away from him and back into the kitchen. She should have felt guilty for hurting him, even accidentally, but she didn't.

"You're cold, Avery," he shouted after her. "You're frigid and cruel. You don't know how to respond to a healthy, virile man, that's your problem. Everybody says so. You're getting a reputation in this town as a cold fish. Why don't you try acting like a woman for a change?"

Act like a woman. The phrase rankled. It was what her father had always said. *The man is the boss. Remember your place. Act like a woman.* Well, she didn't care what everybody said, and she wasn't going to be pushed around by any man. That included Thurmond Spreckles, and it included Cal Buchanon, too, if it came to it. She'd act like a woman all right. Her own woman.

LAWLER COUNTY lay slightly more than two hours distant from the heart of Omaha. But the last seventeen miles to the county seat, the town of Lawler, were twisting and narrow, and Tess's little-used foreign compact chuffed, coughed and rattled.

She was grateful when she finally reached the quiet brick streets of Lawler. She passed by the edge of the college called

The Midwest's Most Beautiful Campus. Its weeping willows were the largest she'd ever seen, and they tossed sinuously in the golden dusk. The peacefulness of the place gave her a pang. It was the sort of college she would have chosen to teach at if she hadn't gone into advertising. Well, she told herself sternly, there was no good thinking of that.

Gargle, clatter, hack-hack-hack, said Tess's little red car. It obviously didn't appreciate willow trees or quiet beauty. She ignored the rattle and kept heading north, passing through the town of Wakefield. She took a county road that led through a long stretch of fields where oats waved in the dusk, soft shadows running through them. She passed several fields of cattle, then a pasture with grazing quarter horses.

If all this belonged to Cal Buchanon, she thought, he had an abnormally large spread for northeast Nebraska. And a diverse one.

Buchanon lived in isolation, she thought uneasily. She'd passed two farmhouses that looked deserted. She was reminded of her family's farm and felt a sharp twinge of regret—a way of life was disappearing. So many farmers had gone under lately that Buchanon might be the only one still living on this back road.

The clean smell of country air stirred a painful nostalgia in her. She tried to wrestle it down. Evening was falling in earnest when at last she saw the mailbox at the end of Buchanon's lane.

The sky had faded to lavender gray. She turned up the lane. *Hack, gasp, rattle,* protested her car. *Thump, thump, thump,* protested her heart. During the trip she had tried not to think of the actual confrontation with Cal Buchanon. Now she could postpone it no longer.

She was about to try to have a calm, reasonable dialogue with an angry and unreasonable man. He was tall, dark, handsome, but he was also pig-headed, uncooperative, and he wanted to sue her agency. He might not even let her in the door. He might chase her off his property with a shotgun. That was probably why he was still single and lived in seclusion—he was a recluse, a crank, a borderline psychopath.

She had convinced herself that his house would be a grim example of American gothic at its most forbidding. Tall and angular, it would look haunted by the uneasy ghosts of long-dead settlers, still sorrowing over the harshness of the land.

When she rounded a bend lined with a tree-break of tall pines, she was almost disappointed to see a sprawling red brick house that looked both modern and cheerful. Light poured out from the immense picture window. A wealth of peonies bloomed before the long expanse of the front porch.

A gold-and-white collie loped out to greet her car, barking half-heartedly and wagging its tail. Tess sensed the dog offered no real danger, and it reminded her vaguely of Robbie, her mother's old Border collie. How she'd wept when her father had given the old dog away when he'd moved them into town. She hadn't let herself think of that for years. She shook the memory away.

With a rattle and a gurgle, the car stopped. A girl on a sorrel quarter horse appeared, coming from behind the house. She was a striking girl, tall and slender, with pale blond hair. Her long-lashed eyes were hauntingly familiar.

The niece, Tess knew instinctively. So this was the accomplished photographer—and equally accomplished liar and forger.

The girl's quick eyes took in Tess's license plate, which showed the car was from Omaha. She leaped off the horse and called the dog to her side. She watched as Tess climbed out of the little car. The girl gave Tess's skirt, blouse and shoes a speedy once-over.

Tess felt rumpled and crumpled after her long day. Still, she sensed the niece approved of her outfit—the white skirt and long-sleeved blouse, belted with black, the black art nouveau necklace and earrings.

The girl tethered the horse and walked toward her. She was pretty, and her smile was disarming. "Hi," she said. "You're from Omaha. You look like the artistic type. Are you from the ad agency that Uncle Cal's so mad at?"

Tess wondered how the niece could be so calm and genial. This girl should be in deep trouble.

"I'm Tess Avery, from the Madigan Advertising Agency. Yes, I want to talk to your uncle. You must be the photographer—Barbara Jane?"

"Barbara Jean," the girl corrected. "But you might as well call me Bunny. *He* does. He doesn't want to admit I'm growing up." She glanced significantly toward the house.

Tess put her hands on her hips and looked at the apparently unrepentant Bunny. "Bunny," she said, "I'm sorry to say this, but you've created a big problem for me. You shouldn't have written that letter. You shouldn't have forged those releases."

Bunny looked both guileless and hurt. She reached down to pat the collie. The collie gave Tess a friendly wag of its tail.

"I didn't mean to cause trouble." Bunny's voice quavered with sincerity. "I just thought he'd be perfect for your calendar. The calendar's for a good cause, isn't it? And everybody thinks he's handsome. Of course, *they* don't have to live with him. I just wanted a chance. I want to be a photographer—more than anything. But *he* thinks I'm stupid." She nodded once more in the direction of the house.

Tess took a deep breath. The darkening air was redolent with the scents of hay and cattle and horses and the fresh west wind, making her perversely homesick. She pulled herself back to the present. "Bunny, I understand your motives. I even sympathize with them. But what you did was wrong—"

Bunny's face grew earnest. "I know that. You don't know how sorry I am. But maybe you can make it right. I mean, I've apologized and apologized, and other people have told him he ought to go ahead and do it—maybe everything can still work out. All I wanted was a professional photography credit. I guess I wanted it too much. Haven't you ever wanted something that much?"

Tess looked at the girl's pleading face. Yes, she understood all too well. She had wanted to get out of her father's narrow little world and into the big world, to do something creative and worthwhile and important, something he believed she couldn't do. She not only sympathized with Bunny; she could identify with her.

Bunny now looked contrite to the point of tears. "I understand," Tess said. "But I don't know if your uncle will even talk to me."

Bunny's spirit bounced back with alacrity. "Oh, he will. I'll see that he does. I'll guarantee it. What's the matter with your car, by the way? That's how I knew you were here. I heard you. Your car sounds like it's going to explode."

"It always sounds that way."

"Gee," Bunny said artlessly, "I thought people in advertising made all kinds of money. Like you'd drive a Corvette or something. Does your agency use a lot of photography? I'd love to get a job as a photographer. And my boyfriend Fred would like a job in advertising, too. He and I are practically soul mates. You know of any openings?"

Tess shook her head. Did this child begin to understand how serious the situation was? "Not right now." She took a deep breath. She had to get down to business. "Look, Bunny, I've got to talk to your uncle, or I might not be with the agency myself any longer. Can you persuade him to see me?"

Bunny nodded. "Sure. Piece of cake. Come on." She started up the stairs.

"You mean I just walk in on him?" Tess felt a surge of nervousness.

"Sure," Bunny said blithely. "Easiest way—corner him. What's he's going to do? Pick you up and carry you back out? He can't do that."

Tess's knees felt jellyish as she followed Bunny up the porch stairs and through the front door. She found herself in a large, airy living room. She looked about warily, as if Cal Buchanon might leap from some niche and pounce on her with a war whoop.

She swallowed. The room was surprisingly homey. Smoke-gray carpeting covered the floor, and a brick fireplace dominated one wall. The overstuffed furniture was upholstered with soft, nubby wine-colored material. The walls were hung with framed photographs. Bunny's work, Tess guessed.

"He isn't here," Bunny informed her. "We've got to go back to the den. This way."

Bunny led her down a hallway, past a dining room and kitchen. A tall woman with a crown of gray braids looked out from the kitchen and gave both Bunny and Tess a disapproving look. "Bunny? Who's this? What's this? What are you doing?"

Bunny paused long enough to reach through the doorway and pluck an apple from a fruit basket on the counter. "No problem. Edna, this is Tess Avery from Omaha. From the advertising agency. Tess, this is my great aunt Edna. She sort of oversees this place."

Tess had the impression that the tall woman was both surprised and disapproving. "*That* advertising agency? Bunny, you can't—"

"Edna, don't worry."

"Bunny! You can't disturb him—he's—"

"I *know* what I'm doing. This is the only way. Your problem, Edna, is you're scared of him. I'm not."

Bunny grabbed Tess's hand and pulled her along. "Don't pay any attention to her. Trust me."

Tess's heart beat like a drum signaling emergency retreat. Bunny pushed open the door and ushered Tess inside. She threw herself down in a blue easy chair next to the stereo and grinned a conspirator's grin.

Tess looked around the room, apprehensive. She saw no sign of Cal Buchanon. The oak-paneled walls were lined with books and framed ribbons from fairs and horse shows. A television stood in the far corner and facing it was a large brown couch, its back to her.

She looked at Bunny questioningly. The girl smiled and gestured toward the couch.

Puzzled, Tess stepped so she could see the front of the couch. She stopped. Her heart also seemed to stop. A tickling sensation played in her throat, and a fluttering one jittered in the pit of her stomach.

There, stretched out on the couch asleep, was Cal Buchanon. He wore faded jeans and a black Western-cut shirt, the sleeves rolled up, the front halfway undone. He must have fallen asleep reading—there was an open book facedown on his chest. One lean hand still grasped it lightly. The book was about something called alternate crops. He had kicked off his boots, and his stockinged feet were propped on the arm of the couch.

His wavy black hair fell over his forehead. His nose was just as straight as in the photo, his cheekbones just as sculpted, the line of his mouth just as intriguing. The dark lashes were so long that they cast shadows. He hadn't shaven today, for stubble shadowed his jaw. It didn't matter. He was still the handsomest man Tess had ever seen. *Well, he's handsome, so what?* she reminded herself. *That was the point, wasn't it? To get his picture and sell calendars. So she could get away to New York.*

Then, to her horror, the sleeping man seemed to tense, as if he sensed he was being watched. She gripped her purse more tightly still.

One of his hazel eyes opened and squinted at her. It was a squint of impressive hostility. He frowned, black brows drawing together. He opened his other eye.

He stared at Tess. She stared at him.

Although he didn't change position, his muscles tautened. She wondered uneasily what was going through his mind. His face had turned rigid.

Cal Buchanon was exhausted, and his first thought was that he was hallucinating. He'd been up all night, trying to save a sick mare. When he'd finally come back to the house, long after the sun was up, he'd been rocked to find his picture in the morning paper, along with a stupid story that said he was going to be a model for some fool calendar. The phone had already started ringing. He told Edna to disconnect it.

It made no difference. People started dropping by just to tease him or congratulate him or simply jabber about the moronic business. He had to keep telling them there was no way he was going to do such a stupid stunt, no way, not now, not ever. Then they'd argue with him. Finally he'd plugged the phone in long enough to call the Madigan Advertising Agency and give them blazes, simply to put an end to the madness for once and for all.

Bunny was hysterical that he wouldn't cooperate. Even though the kid was guilty of half a dozen deceptions, Edna took her side. She was almost in tears herself over the whole mess. It was crazy.

Although he hadn't slept for thirty-two hours, he'd taken refuge in mending fences on the north forty for the rest of the afternoon. Anybody who wanted to hassle him would have to do some hard traveling to find him.

He'd come home six hours later and lain on the couch to read for a moment before supper. He'd been tired enough to die.

Now he wondered groggily if he'd done that—died young, either from exhaustion or from a voodoo curse that Bunny had put on him. A perky looking angel in white was standing there, wide-eyed and ready to escort him to a better world.

Well, the dark eyes were beautiful, and she had a devilish cute crop of red-brown curls for an angel, but he wasn't ready to go to glory yet. He tried to scowl her back to heaven. She wouldn't go.

Still befogged with weariness, he felt a few layers of mist clear from his mind. Something was wrong. The Powers That Be had sent him a city angel, for one thing. She was too blasted chic. She was wearing designer jewelry or whatever they called it. Her makeup was too perfect, even for an angel. In fact, she wasn't an angel at all. She was just a city woman with a lot of curly auburn hair and a funny expression on her face. She looked as if she was afraid he'd bite.

What the devil? he asked himself. This woman was a stranger, and she was in his house staring at him. She was in his own personal private *den,* dammit, and she was standing there watching him *sleep.* He glowered at her harder.

She cleared her throat. "Mr. Buchanon?"

He narrowed his bleary eyes. He rubbed his hand across his stubbled chin. Something struck him as odd about her. Now that he looked more closely, he saw she looked tired and harried. She wore her clothes with a lot of style, but they were crumpled, as if she'd had a long day, and her curls were tousled. He could have sworn she smelled slightly of spaghetti sauce. And while she looked scared of him, what she looked most was guilty.

A dark suspicion crossed his mind. She was from that accursed ad agency. Slowly he rose to a sitting position. That seemed to intimidate her even more. Served her right, he thought. He stood, and she seemed to turn a bit pale. *Good,* he thought bitterly.

He took a step forward, and she took a step backward. He walked toward her until she had backed herself into a corner against the bookshelves. She could move no farther. He put one hand on the shelf beside her, so that his arm formed a barrier she couldn't pass. He leaned down to look into those large brown eyes more closely.

He spoke from between clenched teeth. "Who the hell are you? What are you doing in my house?"

His nearness made Tess's chest constrict. Delia had been right. The man was indeed a tough customer. And Tess had the eerie certainty that, in spite of his question, he knew exactly who she was and why she was there. His eyes, although beautiful, flashed an intimidating blaze of anger.

She tried to keep her voice steady. "I'm Tess Avery of the Madigan Agency. I'm the one who put your picture in the paper. I have to talk to you. But first I want to apologize. There's been a terrible mistake. But we can rectify it."

He brought his face nearer to hers. All she could see were his eyes and the resentful fires glittering in their depths. He hated her. There was no mistaking it. "You just made a second terrible mistake," he said. "Get out of my house. You want to talk, go talk to my lawyer."

Tess's strained nerves prickled with anger. He might have every right to be angry, but he had none to bully her. He wanted to intimidate her, and for an unsettling moment he had. But if he thought he could keep it up, he was dead wrong. She had already handled Thurmond Spreckles today, the world's most impossible man. She would handle Buchanon, too, one way or another.

She squared her jaw. He was so near, the scent of him closed around her with disconcerting intimacy—hay and horses and hot prairie summer. "I don't want to talk to your lawyer. I drove over two hours to get here—after a full day's work. I have to drive two hours back. I'm trying to apologize. All I ask is that you listen."

His eyes flashed even more fiercely. His mouth crooked more dangerously. "Out."

She raised her chin. "No."

Displeasure registered on his face. He was in no mood to confront this woman. And he was in no mood to be defied in his own house. "You get out," he said with precarious evenness, "or I carry you out and dump you in the front yard on your round little bottom."

Now Tess grew truly angry. He might be handsome. But he was also stubborn as a Missouri mule and crude as a billy goat. She raised her forefinger and pointed at his chest. "Touch me and you'll regret you ever met me."

"I already regret it," Cal rumbled. "I told you once, I told you twice, get out of my house. That's the third time."

She smiled at him without mirth, her expression as stubborn as his. "For the third time, no."

Cal emitted a long and ragged sigh of exasperation. Then he did exactly what Bunny said he could not do.

He swung Tess up into his arms and started toward the door of the den. He was really going to throw her out.

Worse, he was strong enough to do a thorough job of it. He was amazingly strong. She was both too startled and too embarrassed to object. Her mouth flew open, but no words came out. She hadn't been so angry or humiliated since the night her father told her to leave home.

Then, while she was still frozen with shock, Cal Buchanon stopped short. He was looking past her and what he saw made him swear. As if in furious displeasure, his arms tightened around her.

CHAPTER THREE

SHE FOLLOWED his gaze and almost jumped when she saw Bunny still draped comfortably in the blue chair, watching them with interest. Cal must have just realized the girl was in the room.

"I really wouldn't do that, Uncle Cal," Bunny said, blinking her large hazel eyes. "I mean it's my fault. I invited her in. I told her you'd talk." She polished her apple.

Cal looked at Bunny. Then he looked again at the woman in his arms. His face darkened with disgust. He might have guessed Bunny was behind this. In fact, he would have guessed it, if he hadn't been so bone tired.

His voice went colder than before. "This is it, Bunny. Go to your room. You're grounded for *two* weeks, not one."

His arms tightened even more unmercifully around Tess, making sure she wouldn't wriggle away. She seemed to be experiencing a dozen contradictory emotions at once. Mixed with her anger and embarrassment was an odd tingle of excitement at being imprisoned in this man's arms. She hated the sensation and fought it down.

Tears sprang into Bunny's eyes. "Two weeks? Why don't you just send me to prison? All right—I know you hate me. But what happened is my fault, not Miss Avery's. You shouldn't take it out on her. But you just—you just never listen to anybody—"

Bunny burst into tears and fled, slamming the door behind her.

Cal squeezed Tess even harder against him as he stared at the door. She could feel the pounding of his heart against her shoulder, the angry rise and fall of his hard chest. He looked down at her, his expression as unfriendly as ever. Emotions warred on his handsome, stubborn, weary face.

"All right." The distaste in his voice bit into her like acid. "You want to talk? Talk. I'll give you five minutes. What do you want to say?"

Tess gazed at him as if he were insane. "The first thing I'd like to say, Mr. Buchanon, is please put me *down*."

He blinked and frowned slightly. He'd had so many unpleasant surprises in the past forty-eight hours and so little sleep that he was letting small details slip by him. He was, indeed, still holding the woman.

For the first time it occurred to him that she felt pleasant in his arms, soft, warm and curving. This was the last sort of thought he should have. He set her down as swiftly as if she'd been made of fire.

Each of them took a step backward from the other.

"Sorry," he said, which surprised her. "I was up all night. Sick mare."

He ran his hand over his face as if to scrub away the fatigue. For the first time Tess realized she was dealing with a man who was dead on his feet. She would have to treat him carefully.

She straightened her blouse, adjusted her earring nervously. "Look, I'm sorry, too. I'm sure this came as a shock to you. It did to the agency, too. We had no intention of violating your privacy, we thought the releases were genuine—"

He turned away from her and leaned his elbow on one of the bookshelves. He frowned at the volumes without seeing them. "The damage is done. Don't do any more. Just print a retraction." He bent his head and massaged his temples with the thumb and middle finger of his right hand.

"Mr. Buchanon—" Tess took a step toward him. "We'll print a retraction if you insist. But what we'd rather do is have you sign an actual release for those photos. Mrs. Madigan, the head of the agency, thinks you'd be an invaluable addition to the calendar project—"

His head snapped up. He glared at her. "I won't be on any damned calendar."

She took a deep breath, praying for patience and tact. The man was angry, stubborn and bone weary, and she wasn't at her best, either. This wasn't going to be easy. "Mr. Buchanon, the project isn't what you probably think. You don't even have to pose—the picture's already been taken. It's not a—a revealing picture. You're not supposed to look—well, sexy or anything. It's not as if we are asking you to take off your clothes—"

He snorted in derision. "You're not going to ask me to take off my clothes? Am I supposed to be thankful for small favors? Great—I won't ask you to take off your clothes, either. Oh, maybe just your blouse. I had my shirt off. Fair's fair, after all."

He stared frankly at the thrust of her breasts against the thin white material of her blouse. He raised one eyebrow in speculation. She blushed but tried not to let his appraisal rattle her any worse that he already had. "I didn't mean to insult you—"

He hit the flat of his palm against the bookshelf. "You already did. I won't be on any blasted calendar. Don't even think about it."

Tess held her hands out, fingers spread in supplication. "It's not an insult—it's actually an honor. And it's for a wonderful cause. The Homestead Heritage Foundation wants to raise money to help the small farmers and ranchers of this state."

He hit the bookcase again and turned his gaze from her in disgust. "I know what Homestead Heritage is and what it wants. I also know that no stupid calendar is going to save anybody in this state. The problem's too big—the whole farm economy's changing.''

Tess knew he was right, but it was her job to persuade him otherwise. ''It's a problem we can solve a step at a time. The calendar is one small step.''

''The calendar is one big asinine piece of hype and hoopla. Homestead Heritage ought to be having seminars, educating people about diversifying crops, not printing a lot of idiotic calendars.''

Tess shook her head in perplexity. ''Lots of people have expressed interest—''

''No. Flat out no.''

''Would you listen with an open mind for just one minute?''

He shot her a look that almost quelled her. ''I don't have to listen to you at all. This is my house. You listen to me. I want a retraction. Say you'll make it, and then go. The door is right behind you.''

Tess exhaled sharply. She tossed a wayward curl from her eyes. ''I know you're upset, but rudeness doesn't help, Mr. Buchanon.''

His expression became one of irritable disbelief. ''You smear my picture all over the state—you come walking right into my house. You creep up on me while I'm asleep on my own couch. And *you* object because *I'm* rude?''

They glowered at each other. Tess forced herself not to think of him as attractive. He was an obstacle, that was all, an obstacle to her career. And he was a large and powerful one, as full of fury as a storm cloud.

Someone knocked at the door. ''Come in,'' Cal snapped. He stopped glaring at Tess and instead glared at the door. It opened and a man's round, smiling face appeared. His blue eyes darted from Tess to Cal, and his smile faded slightly.

"Hello, Cal," the man said. "I hope I'm not interrupting. Do you have a moment? I'd like to talk to you."

Cal looked up at the ceiling as if it might deliver some badly needed patience into his hands. Then he managed to give the man a tight-lipped smile. "Good evening, Reverend Yonke."

Tess looked at the chubby little man and inwardly groaned. Reverend Yonke wore a clergyman's collar. He was bald except for a neat fringe of brown hair, and his smooth face was, fittingly, as bland as a cherub's. A small-town minister was the last person that she needed. He would disapprove of the calendar project on principle.

Cal forced himself to become civil. It obviously took great effort. "Reverend Bob Yonke, this is Miss Avery. She's from Omaha. She's just leaving. Aren't you, Miss Avery?"

Reverend Yonke beamed at Tess and shook her hand. "I'm pleased to meet you, Miss Avery. You represent the ad agency? The calendar project? That's what Edna said. I didn't mean to barge in on you...."

"Sit down, Reverend," Cal said. He put his hands on his hips. The pose made him look extremely determined. "Don't worry. You're not interrupting. And I don't intend to do anything to embarrass the parish. I just told Miss Avery here that I have no intention of being on any calendar."

There, his sidelong look at Tess seemed to smirk. *I've got a man of God on my side. Go away, will you?*

Reverend Yonke sat down on the brown couch. His smile didn't waver. "But Cal," he said, shaking his head, "that's what I've come to talk about. I think you should. Be on the calendar, that is."

Cal's expression lost its triumphant set. Tess's mouth fell open again. She stared in amazement at Reverend Yonke.

"You what?" Cal's voice was toneless.

"I came to ask you to be on the calendar. Edna called me—" Yonke shot a happy glance at Tess "—that's Cal's Aunt Edna, and she said that you, Cal, never agreed to be on the calendar. That you weren't going to agree."

Cal leaned his elbow on the bookshelf again. There were shadows under his eyes, and his mouth was drawn down at the corners. "Did Edna tell you what Bunny did? That she forged my signature and sent those pictures in? Listen, Reverend, if only for that reason, I wouldn't be on that calendar—I'm not going to encourage Bunny."

"But Bunny needs encouragement," Reverend Yonke said, beaming even more earnestly. "You know, Edna and I were talking only last week about Bunny. She's a good child at heart, you know. She simply marches to a different drummer."

"She marches to a different heavy metal band," Cal said darkly. "And she's got Edna wrapped around her little finger. She always has. Bunny's got to learn—"

"I agree." Revered Yonke nodded. "She's got to learn to respect and love herself. She isn't like the other two. She's a much more restless little soul. What gives her the most sense of her own worth is her photography. And Edna thinks that she must be encouraged to do what she does best. It's the only way to channel all that vibrant young energy."

"The other two?" Tess asked, intrigued. She vaguely remembered that Bunny was one of three children. Caught up in the moment, she had forgotten she was an uninvited and unwanted guest in the Buchanon house.

Cal's cold glance told her the question was none of her business.

Reverend Yonke eyed Cal proudly, then turned to Tess. "The other two children, Marissa and John. Cal raised all three of them when his sister died. That's one of the reasons the community would be proud for him to represent us. He was only twenty-four years old when he took on this farm—and all three children. Marissa's married now, and John's finishing college. Cal's done a splendid job."

"Lately Bunny has hardly been an example of splendid upbringing." Cal's voice was laced with sarcasm.

"It's a phase," the reverend replied. "She's asserting her independence. You're strict with her, Cal."

"I have to be. Do you realize she wants to go out with that bozo from the college? That he's ten years older than she is?"

The reverend gave a little sigh. He raised his shoulders manfully. "I know. Edna's worried, too. That's why she wants to make sure Bunny's happy at home. Cal, you and Bunny will work things out, and the first thing is solving this calendar dispute. At first Edna was worried what people would think if you did cooperate—she called me. Well, I've talked informally to all the church elders. We think you should reconsider your decision. This calendar project will bring a lot of needed aid to small farmers. You mustn't hide your light under a bushel. We've all seen the photograph. It represents an ideal—a man of the land protecting one of the creatures in his care. Bunny captured the spirit wonderfully. Yes, Cal, we want to ask you to participate—and do so proudly. You're too shy and modest, my boy. Do it, for our sakes and with our blessing."

Tess bit her lip. Cal looked at once so furious and so stunned that a muscle in his cheek jumped, as if he could barely keep it in control. The black brows lowered. He gave the reverend a long, wary look. "You and the church elders actually want me to do this damn—excuse me—this fool stunt?"

The reverend nodded. Although he seemed cheerful and bland, Tess sensed a will of absolute iron behind his smiling facade. He had made up his mind about what was right, and that was that. "Your ranch here is successful. Now you have an opportunity to help others less fortunate than yourself."

Cal pushed his hair back from his forehead as if his skull ached abominably. "Greater love hath no man than he lay down every scrap of his dignity, is that it?"

The reverend stood. He walked to Cal's side, put his hand on the younger man's broad shoulder. "Dignity comes from within, Cal. A mere picture can't affect it. You take things so seriously. You've always had to. Look on this as having a bit of fun. Heaven knows you could do with some. You've had a great many responsibilities for a very long time."

"Fun," Cal said bleakly. He looked down at the little man in the clerical collar. He made it a point to ignore Tess, who still stood, staring at the two of them, her hands clenched together.

There was a soft knock at the door. It opened again. Cal's Aunt Edna appeared, looking around its edge. "Cal, Bunny's sorry, she really is. I found her out in back, crying her heart out, poor thing. She wanted to apologize in front of everyone."

She opened the door more widely. Bunny, her eyes red and swollen from weeping, stood behind Edna. "I'm sorry," she said. "And I'll understand if you won't be on the calendar. I *should* be punished. I like to pretend I'm good at taking pictures, but—I know I never do anything to make you proud of me. Can you forgive me?" She stepped forward, her head down, the picture of penitence.

Edna's handsome face tensed with expectation. She stood with one hand on Bunny's shoulder. She stared imploringly at her nephew.

Cal's mouth slanted down at one corner. He jammed his hands in the back pocket of his jeans. "All right," he muttered. "I forgive you. And I am proud of you—just not for this particular prank, that's all."

"Oh, Uncle Cal." Bunny burst into tears again. She ran across the room and threw herself into his arms. He embraced her, patting her awkwardly.

He did not look like a happy man. But Tess was touched in spite of herself. The troubled look on his face showed he might really care for the girl. But it also seemed to say that he didn't understand his niece and that perhaps he never could. She remembered how her own father had tried to crush her ambitions. She remembered, too, how Cal had bullied her. She forced away any twinge of sympathy for him.

"Cal—" Reverend Yonke used his most persuasive tone "—for the child's good—for the community's good—would you reconsider being on the calendar?"

Edna nodded. Nervously she smoothed the gray braids that crowned her head. "Cal, it's for a good cause. A wonderful cause. And it means so much to Bunny that her work was accepted."

Tess held her breath. Cal kept Bunny locked in an embrace that was both protective and embarrassed. He looked unused to such displays. Bunny sobbed silently against his neck. His expression turned as grim as that of a man about to be hanged. He looked over Bunny's shoulder, anger and resentment smoldering in his eyes. His gaze met Tess's.

An uneasy silence weighted the room. "It is better to give than to receive, Cal. God loveth a cheerful giver," Reverend Yonke said. "You've run your place well, and it's in no danger, but not all of your neighbors are so lucky. Think how much Bunny's photograph might help them."

Cal's arms stayed wrapped around Bunny, and his eyes stayed locked with Tess's, sheer dislike burning in them. Bunny's crying had softened at last.

"Please?" said Edna nervously touching her again. "Please? It *is* a good cause, Cal."

He gave his aunt a look of exasperation. "It's a lost cause. But if it's the only way I can keep everybody off my back—and get some sleep—all right. I'll do it."

His eyes, haggard and angry, returned to Tess, drilling into her. Bunny might be forgiven. But she was not.

"Use the stupid pictures," Cal told Tess. "Who cares?"

The bitterness in his voice showed that he cared, and cared a great deal. Reverend Yonke smiled so widely that Tess could see his back teeth. Edna twisted her hands together, her smile shy. Cal's face only grew stonier.

"I love you, Uncle Cal," Bunny said, kissing his shadowed cheek. Tess's heart gave an unexpected little lurch, and she admonished it to behave. "You're the best uncle in the world. And you probably saved Miss Avery's job."

Bunny turned and grinned at Tess. "Want me to photograph the other men? I'd do a good job, I promise. And I'd work cheap."

"Bunny! You're *not* going to go around photographing strange men." Cal's admonition was so harsh that even Reverend Yonke jumped. Cal glanced again at Tess, who stood wide-eyed. She could feel his unvoiced accusation, as forceful as an assault: *this is all your fault—somehow.* If he could no longer blame Bunny, then Tess would be the target of his wrath.

"Well, this is a happy development indeed," said Reverend Yonke. "I won't take up any more of your evening, Cal. I have the feeling that great good will come out of this. Many unfortunate farmers and ranchers can be helped. It's been nice to meet you, Miss Avery. Cal, here, will make a worthy subject for your calendar. Hard to find a finer man. Oh, he might try to frighten you with those severe looks of his sometimes, but he's a fine man, a fine man."

"I'll walk you and Miss Avery to your cars," the fine man said sourly. "You're leaving, aren't you, Miss Avery? It's a long drive back to Omaha."

"About the releases—" Tess began. She wanted them signed before he changed his mind. He seemed in such a volatile mood that anything might happen.

"Just leave them with me. I'll sign them and have them in the mail for you tomorrow," he muttered. "Bunny, as I recall, knows how to fill the forms out." He gave Bunny a sideways glance.

"Well—" Tess laughed nervously. "I'd feel safer if you'd sign them now. Everything's been so upsy-downsy about this business...."

"Tomorrow." Cal took her by the elbow and propelled her out the door of the den. Edna and Bunny followed, Edna arm in arm with Reverend Yonke.

"But—" Tess tried to protest.

"Tomorrow." He snapped the word out sharply, as if he were cocking the hammer of a gun.

"You don't have to steer me out of your house," Tess objected. His touch bothered her. It was insulting for one thing. But there was something else that disturbed her, something to which she did not want to give a name.

"I want to make sure you're out. Don't worry. I don't enjoy touching you, if that's what worries you. I mean, you're all right, but frankly you smell like—like spaghetti sauce."

Tess flashed him a resentful glance. "That's because I spent the afternoon working with another big ape." She almost bit her tongue. She should have held her temper. She didn't need to make the man any angrier.

"Not funny," he said leading her out the front door. "And it doesn't explain why you smell like a plate of pasta. Is that the latest thing in the big city?"

"I can't help it. I did spend all day with an ape—shooting a commercial about cooking spaghetti. I had to come straight here from there." *And the ape's manners, Mr.*

Buchanon, were far better than yours, she thought rebelliously.

His mouth went cynical. "Why make the poor ape cook? Raising money for the underprivileged spaghetti chefs of Nebraska? Or the jobless monkeys?"

He was ushering her down the stairs too speedily for comfort. She tried to wrench her elbow away. "It happens to be a charming commercial. It's for Pasquerali's restaurant. The slogan is 'Pasquerali's—we don't monkey around.'"

"How profound. You must be proud to spread such a meaningful message." He opened the door of her car and waited impatiently for her to get in.

He had hit her where it hurt most, but she refused to flinch. She'd learned to defend the silly things she often had to do in her work. "Our agency happens to be extremely good, Mr. Buchanon. We win a lot of awards."

"Right," he said sarcastically. "For monkeyshines. Goodbye, Miss Avery. Have a good trip."

Tess shook her head at his rudeness and got into the car. He closed the door firmly, as if afraid she would escape from it and return to haunt him.

He turned his back and began to stalk away. He paused to wave to Reverend Yonke, whose small car was already putt-putting down the lane. Edna and Bunny stood together, also waving after the car.

Tired and frustrated, Tess stuck her key into the ignition. She wanted to put as much distance between herself and Cal Buchanon as possible. He might be handsome, but he was as prickly as a porcupine, and she was glad she'd never have to see his face again except on the stupid calendar. He was a disturbing man, and in too many ways his relationship with Bunny reminded her of her own with her father. She was anxious to flee the whole complicated scene. She turned the key in the ignition and stepped on the gas.

Nothing happened.

The car made a feeble *wank-wanking* noise, warning lights flickered feebly on the dashboard, but nothing else came to life.

She tried again.

Wank, wank, wank, croaked the engine. Then it went ominously silent.

Darn! thought Tess. For months the old car had been threatening to betray her. Now it had done so. She sat in the Nebraska darkness, listening to the night around her almost echo with emptiness.

She stepped on the gas pedal once more.

The car sniveled, whined, then settled back into its frightening silence.

She felt Cal walking back toward her. She didn't have to look up. She could sense the displeasure radiating from him as palpably as if he were hurling thunderbolts at her.

He put his hand on the edge of the window. She could see it out of the corner of her eye. She clenched her teeth and tried to start the car again. Nothing.

"What is this?" He almost hissed the words, such was his hostility.

She refused to look at him. "It won't start."

"Is this some kind of trick?"

She whirled to face him. His shadowy face looked hard in the faint moonlight. "Trick? I have to be at work tomorrow morning. I don't want to be stuck in the hinterlands with you and the moo-cows, Mr. Buchanon. Nothing could appeal to me less." She was too unsettled to pretend to be polite.

"You probably flooded the engine," he grumbled. "Get out. Let me try."

Grudgingly she climbed out of the car. His shoulder brushed hers as he got in. They both flinched away from the accidental contact. A tingle jolted through her arm and ran down her spine and back up again. *I could really hate you,* she thought.

He tried the engine once, he tried it twice, and then he swore. Tess sighed in exhaustion and folded her arms on the roof of the car. She buried her face in her arms.

She'd have to ask this disagreeable lunk to get her to a motel somehow. Then she'd have to pay for the motel and car repairs—who knew how much that might cost?—and she'd lose at least a day's work. She couldn't afford that. The payment on her college loan was due, and besides, she didn't want to make a bad impression on Mrs. Madigan, who was a harsh taskmistress.

He got out and slammed the door so hard the little car shook. Tess bit her lip as he began to stride toward the house. Edna reached a hand out, stopping him. "Cal? What's wrong?"

"I don't know," he said shortly. "I think it's her water pump."

Edna shook her head in concern. "Oh, dear. What will you do?"

"Call Harv at the garage. He'll have to tow her in. He can drop Miss Avery off at the motel in Wakefield."

"Oh, Cal, you can't do that—it's late, and we have plenty of room. She can stay here, with us."

Cal glanced back at Tess. Even in the darkness she felt the cold distaste in his look.

He opened his mouth to give Edna an emphatic "no," but Bunny had already sprinted to Tess's side and seized her by the elbow. "You'll stay with us, won't you? Why go to a motel when we've got plenty of room? We owe you that— it's my fault you drove clear up here. Edna doesn't mind. Really!"

Cal opened his mouth again, but Edna gave him a pleading look. "Cal," she said, "you're very, very tired. You're not yourself. Please. It's the only neighborly thing to do."

Edna moved to Bunny's side and put her arm around her grandniece. Her voice, like her face, radiated sincerity. "Miss Avery, we have plenty of room, and Bunny's right. We're the reason you had to make this long drive. It would be no trouble to have you stay. I like doing for people."

Edna was as gracious as her nephew was short-tempered, and Tess instinctively liked her. She even liked Bunny—although the girl was troublesome, she was also vulnerable, creative and full of life. It was Cal, the Grump of the Western World, who set her on edge.

"Stay with us," Edna urged. "Please. Do."

"Yes," Bunny begged. "Please."

Tess shook her head. She watched Cal's shadowy figure, silhouetted under a maple tree. He was looking out over the starry meadow, as if he could shut out the women's existence. "I don't think Mr. Buchanon wants me to stay. I wouldn't feel comfortable."

Edna reached out to pat Tess's hand. "Cal's not hardhearted. He's just independent, and he doesn't like giving in. You've seen him at his worst. It'd be nice for you to give him another chance."

"I'm going in the house," Cal said, "I'm going to bed. You people do whatever you want. Leave me out of it." He walked away.

"You see," Tess said. "He resents me."

"He resents all creative women," Bunny said, her chin held rebelliously high.

"Bunny!" There was shock in Edna's gentle voice. "You were just telling him how grateful you were and how much you love him."

"I do love him, and I'm grateful to him, but I know he resents creative women. That's why we fight all the time. I remind him of my mother. And he hates it. That's why I adore Fred. He's not threatened by somebody who does something original."

"Bunny!" Edna admonished. She turned to Tess again. "Don't mind us, Miss Avery. We've had a trying day. And we've made you have one. Do us the honor of being our guest. Perhaps we'll look better in the light of a new day. It's the least we can do, and it would give me pleasure."

Tess hesitated. The invitation seemed to be offered with both kindness and honesty.

Bunny cocked her head wryly. "Besides, we can't get you to a motel. Cal's gone to bed, Edna hates to drive at night, and I'm grounded. You have to stay."

Tess looked at the two women in dismay.

Edna nodded sheepishly. "It's true. My night vision is scandalous. And Cal's forbidden Bunny to drive for the next week."

"The next two weeks." Bunny's tone returned to glum.

Tess stood, letting the night wind caress her. She felt disoriented and helpless. She tried to shrug, as if nothing of consequence were at stake. "I guess you have yourselves a houseguest."

"Great," Bunny said. "Come on in. I'll show you your room. I'll loan you a nightgown and give you a toothbrush and stuff."

"Would you like some milk and pie? Or perhaps a glass of sherry?" Edna asked. "Maybe even a little supper? I could heat something up for you."

"No thanks." Tess shook her head, wishing she didn't feel quite so dazed.

For the first time in years, she was going to spend the night on a farm. The prospect both excited and frightened her. Her emotions were far more complex than she wished to admit. All sorts of feelings had reawakened in her, ones she had long suppressed. They surged through her so strongly she felt almost dizzied.

Standing in the warm dark, she sensed that nothing seemed quite real. After struggling for years to escape rural

Nebraska, she was suddenly back, stranded in its very heart. It was as if time had suddenly run backward, marooning her on the moonlit plains.

All day life had taken on a quality that veered between strange nightmare and even stranger dream. Now she was about to spend the night under the same roof with the handsomest man in Nebraska. He had also proved to be the most disagreeable and pig-headed man in Nebraska. He made her blood course with resentment, but with an unexpected excitement, too. It was the excitement that troubled her most. She didn't want to feel it. She didn't like it.

The dark wind sighed, the crickets chirped, and a cicada made its whirring noise. Somewhere a cow lowed. It all sounded so familiar and brought so many memories pouring back from her childhood that Tess's soul ached.

Her heart beating hard and her throat tight, she followed Bunny into Cal Buchanon's house.

CHAPTER FOUR

THE GUEST ROOM was a large, airy bedroom that Tess supposed must have once belonged to the other niece, Marissa. It seemed too incontestably feminine to exist otherwise near Cal Buchanon's presence.

The long, ruffled curtains at the wide window were white, sprigged with blue flowers and tied back with blue sashes. The matching spread on the four-poster bed was lavishly ruffled as well. The bed itself was double, made of brass, but unlike many brass beds its lines were delicate rather than heavy. The floor was oak, polished to the color of gold and scattered with hooked rugs.

On the wall behind the bed hung a cluster of pictures. A white-and-blue china hurricane lamp on the bedside table shined as if in welcome.

The window was open, the curtains fluttering gently. The mild night breeze carried the pungent odor of seasoned hay and the soft, creaking sound of crickets.

Tess stood motionless a moment, hugging Bunny's nightgown and robe to her chest. The room was lovely, the kind most girls would dream of having, rich yet homey. It looked as if it had been both well used and well loved.

But, although she was unaccustomed to such a beautiful room, it gave her an odd feeling. It was as if she was not in this place for the first time, but was returning to it after a long absence. She recognized the deep and abiding peace of the country night, the comforting quiet that she knew from childhood and that was bred into her very bones.

She shook her head, set the nightclothes on the dresser and ran her hand over her tousled hair. She'd forgotten how long it had been since she'd heard both the countryside's sounds and its silence, had inhaled its clean and honest scent. Her apartment in Omaha was near a busy street and she was used to the rumble of traffic all night long, the smell of exhaust fumes hanging in the air.

I don't miss this. I don't, Tess told herself, squeezing her eyes shut. She shook her head again to clear it. She was tired, that was all, confused and tired.

Squaring her shoulders, she opened her eyes. She stepped beside the bed and examined the pictures on the wall. In each of them was a pretty, happy-faced girl with dark hair and Cal Buchanon's long-lashed eyes. Marissa, Tess thought. In some of the photos, she recognized a younger Bunny, staring at the camera as if thinking very hard. And in two were Cal.

Tess drew in her breath again. In one photograph he was at least ten years younger, and so, of course, were the dark-haired girl and Bunny. He must have been in his middle twenties, and he had one arm around Marissa's shoulders. She, thin, leggy and no more than fifteen, looked up at him with adoration. In his other arm, he held Bunny. Bunny was no more than five, and she looked as if she was crying. Cal was looking at Bunny.

Drat, but he *was* a handsome man, Tess thought. In his twenties, he had been almost as handsome as he was now. His shoulders were just as broad, his hips as slim, but his face then had been a bit smoother, unlined and less mature.

The expression on that face was what was truly arresting, however. He was smiling. The smile was the gentle, jesting one that kindly adults use when they are trying to cheer unhappy children. Bunny's expression was cranky and tearful, but Cal, holding her, looked concerned enough to stop any child's tears.

Tess forced her eyes away from the photo. She didn't want to think about a tender side of him. The man was only a problem, an obstacle to her. She turned her attention to the other picture of him and Marissa.

In this more recent photo, Marissa wore her college cap and gown and held a diploma. Cal's dark suit was of an expensive cut, and he wore it well, looking more like an executive than a rancher. He was hugging Marissa, laughing down at her. Both of them radiated pride and love, and Tess looked away from that picture, too.

Don't start thinking of him as a nice man, she warned herself. *He doesn't think of you as a nice woman, and he's not likely to.* Besides, she thought, what would she want with some man stuck out on a patch of Nebraska land that froze all winter and parched all summer? Nothing. She had left that kind of life behind forever.

She stripped off her clothes and took a quick shower in Marissa's small but gleaming bathroom. Then she slipped into Bunny's nightgown, a long white cotton one with eyelet straps and matching trim along the bodice.

Because Tess was more curvaceous than Bunny, her breasts swelled against the straight-cut bodice, and she cocked a rueful eyebrow at her reflection in the mirror. Thurmond Spreckles, lust in his eye as usual, had once told her that she had the breasts of a goddess. She was glad he wasn't here to see them practically thrusting out of Bunny's gown.

She turned back the bedspread and lace-edged sheet. Slipping into bed, she turned off the lamp. With a weary sigh she sank against the pillow and closed her eyes.

An hour later she still was not asleep. Sleep seemed, in fact, so impossible to attain that she started to wonder if Cal had cursed her and she would never sleep again.

She didn't know if her restlessness was because of the strange bed or because of the familiar sounds and scents of the night. Even the bed sheets brought back memories. They smelled of sunshine and prairie wind, the way sheets used to smell when she was a child and her mother hung them out on the line to dry, and they had the same clean, crispy feel.

She signed and raised herself on one elbow. She told herself that her day had been so horrible it had given her insomnia. In her mind, chimpanzees were still juggling meatballs, Thurmond Spreckles still stalked her, and Cal Buchanon still glowered, refusing to sign a release for his photographs.

Too many crises at work, Tess told herself, and a stalled car as well, to say nothing of being marooned in the boondocks. No wonder she was restless.

Somewhere out in the darkness, a distant cow lowed and another answered. The breeze carried the sounds to her like ghosts from the past. How many nights had she gone to sleep to those haunting but comforting sounds, she wondered. How many years had it been?

I can't stand this,, she told herself irritably. *Some stupid cow moos, and I'm off like a crazy woman, running down memory lane. I hate it.*

She sat up, running her fingers through her curls. Perhaps, she thought with a sense of fatalism, she should stop resisting and just let herself plunge into useless nostalgia and get it out of her system.

Well, she thought, she might as well do it right. There had been an old-fashioned swing on the front porch. She would go out, sit in it, and let all the old sensations assault her full force. She would challenge them, face them, vanquish them for once and for all. Then she would tell them goodbye. She was leaving all this behind soon, and she wasn't coming back.

She rose and, without switching on the light, put on Bunny's long white cotton robe, leaving the belt untied. She opened the door as quietly as possible. A night-light in the hall cast the faintest of glows to guide her steps into the front of the house.

The drapes were open in the big front room, and moonlight poured through the sheer curtains of the picture window. Moonlight silvered everything in the room and gave it a slightly enchanted look.

She moved to the front door and eased it open. She stepped outside and closed it soundlessly behind her. The bricks of the porch were cool beneath her bare feet.

The night was awash with moonlight, the sky almost opalescent with it. She stared up at the sky, relishing its cleanness and limitlessness. The stars were so thick they spilled in clouds across it.

Can the sky be as beautiful anywhere else? Tess wondered with a pang. It had been years since she'd seen the night sky like this.

The air was so fresh it made her tingle inside and out. The crickets sang, and the breeze stirred in the peony bushes and the branches of the weeping willow trailing the front lawn.

Tess leaned on the porch railing and inhaled deeply. The breeze played over her, stirring her hair and making the loose robe flutter. These were the sweet scents of her childhood, these were its beautiful moon-washed sights.

Oh, she thought, it had been such a hard life, but so lovely in its way. She had wept her heart out when her father had made them leave the farm. She had thought then that this was the only way that people were meant to live, next to the land and at peace with it.

But people couldn't always stay at peace with one another, she thought darkly, remembering her father. And the land, for all its beauty, could be cruel enough to kill.

She turned away from the moon-drenched lawn, the faint breeze making the open robe billow lightly around her. Moving toward the porch swing, she stared out moodily toward the barn and outbuildings. With a sigh she sat down, nestling against the swing's low back. She closed her eyes and listened to the cricket's broken song.

"What in *hell* are you doing?" a voice growled, practically in her ear. "Or are you on twenty-four-hour alert to ruin my life?"

Tess gave such a physical start it was almost violent. She whirled to look over her shoulder.

Cal Buchanon stood directly behind the swing. The moonlight glazed his high cheekbones and the strong line of his jaw. The breeze tousled the black hair that fell across his brow and stirred the collar of his dark shirt.

"What are you doing here?" Tess demanded. Her heart galloped so hard that it made her voice unsteady.

"I *live* here," he said, with the acid of satire. "I came out onto *my* porch to sit in *my* swing. You, incidentally, have my spot. Move over."

Hastily Tess slid to the other side of the swing, pulling the robe tightly shut. She watched warily as he stepped from behind and sat. She gave a slight involuntary shudder at his nearness. She said nothing.

He did not speak, either. He leaned his head back, his face tilted up slightly, and closed his eyes. He was probably imagining, Tess thought uneasily, that she wasn't there.

His profile, silhouetted by the moonlight, was so perfect that she found it irritating. He gave off the slightly minty scent of soap, and his hair shone with dampness. A fresh shirt of dark blue or black stretched across his chest, and his long legs were clad in dark jeans. He had obviously showered and changed since she had seen him last. She wondered, apprehensively, why he was still awake.

He stretched his legs out and crossed his feet at the ankles. His black cowboy boots gleamed dully in the pearly light. One arm lay on that of the swing, his lean hand dangling down. He raised his other elbow and rested it on the swing's back. His hand almost brushed Tess's shoulder. He didn't bother to open his eyes, but his mouth took on an unhappy quirk.

"You followed me out here, didn't you?" he asked, his voice emotionless.

Tess's head snapped back a fraction of an inch in displeased surprise. She tied the belt of the robe, knotting it tightly. "Follow you? I wouldn't follow you. You came creeping up on me."

He kept his eyes closed. "I was standing there in plain sight. On the other side of the porch."

"Right," Tess countered. "In the shadows. Dressed all in dark colors. Like a ninja or something."

He yawned.

Good grief, thought Tess in disgust, he was even handsome when he yawned, stretched out like a lounging cat.

"Sorry," he said. "I'm not really interested in socializing."

"Who asked to socialize?" she asked tartly.

"You're here aren't you?" His voice was sarcastic. "That's socializing."

Tess refused to be intimidated. "I'm making no demands."

His eyes stayed closed, but he grimaced slightly. "Yes, you are. You're making demands on my time, my patience, my dignity and my family. I think I could take it all, except the demands on the family. I don't like what you're making happen. Every time you're around, warning bells go off in my head."

"Is that what kept you awake?" she asked out of the corner of her mouth. "The bells in your head? Sorry. I didn't mean to ring your chimes. I'm really quite harmless."

"I doubt that."

"If you're so tired, and I'm so irritating," she said, "why don't you just go to bed and go to sleep?"

He didn't move. He stayed as motionless as a statue, his eyes still shut. The weariness in his voice was tinged with mockery. "I tried. I'm too tired to sleep. Unlike you, however, I put some clothes on before I came out. I guess I'm just an old-fashioned guy. Boring, huh?"

Tess hugged herself more tightly into the thin robe. The night no longer seemed warm. Cal's presence made a chill go prickling along her skin. She forced herself to take her eyes away from him and to stare off at the moon-dazzled horizon.

"I couldn't sleep, either," she said.

The sardonic slant returned to his mouth. "It's too quiet. You're not used to it. That's what city people always say."

"I'm more used to it than I want to be," she retorted. "Don't try to cast me in the role of the city slicker. I grew up on a farm."

He turned his head slightly. He opened one eye. "You? Ha." He closed the eye and turned his face away once more.

Tess bristled. "What's that supposed to mean? 'Ha'?"

"Ha. It means 'Ha.'"

"I did. A farm in Frontier County."

"You don't sound happy about it," he said.

She made her voice as cold as possible. "I'm not particularly."

He sighed as if he found the subject of little interest. "Care to tell me why?"

"No," she returned. "Actually I wouldn't." Too many painful memories and unruly emotions were already stirring within her.

"Do you want me to guess?"

"No. I don't."

He gave a rough sigh and settled more comfortably into the swing's cushions. "I'll try anyway. Why'd a sweet young thing like you leave the farm? Let's see. You wanted bright lights, big city. The brighter and bigger, the better."

She looked away, stung. A surprising acrimony had edged his voice.

He wasn't precisely accurate, but she wouldn't give him the satisfaction of an argument. "Right," she said from between her teeth.

He went on in the same bored, bitter voice. "But Omaha can't hold the likes of you. You've got your sights set on someplace with more glitter—right? New York? L.A.? Chicago?"

Reluctantly she let her gaze return to him, wondering how he could tell such a thing. He was still stretched out, eyes shut. She regarded him with wariness and puzzlement. "New York. How did you know?"

"I've seen it all before." He yawned again.

That yawn told her with languid eloquence just how uninteresting he found her. Anger prickled through her.

"You have second sight?" she asked acidly. "The gift of prophecy?"

"Just eyes," he said and rubbed his tiredly with the thumb and forefinger of his right hand. "I watched your face tonight. It was the face of a someone who sees her life spinning down the drain. You looked desperate. Like your future was at stake. It was clear—from the way you dress, the way you look, the way you are—you're a woman trying to get someplace. You were afraid I was going to stop you. It scared you sick."

She straightened her back, held her chin higher. She remembered how Bunny had said he resented creative women. So this was his flaw, she thought with animosity—he was an old-fashioned, hard-line male chauvinist, just like her father and brothers. "What's so wrong with a woman 'trying to get someplace'?"

He shrugged as if the question didn't interest him. "Nothing. As long as she doesn't step on people getting there. Or mess up her own life. Getting somewhere is fine. Just fine."

He lapsed back into silence, looking as if he were trying to fall asleep. She stared at him in frustration. "Then what's your problem? Because you certainly don't sound as if you approve of me. And I've done nothing."

His eyes opened. He stared stonily toward the roof of the porch. "The problem," he said, "is you were trying to step on *me.*"

Tess tossed him a resentful glance, which he ignored. She might have been the sorriest and humblest of insects, for all the attention he cared to pay her. "I wasn't trying to step on you," she said. "I was trying to get you to cooperate on a charitable project that's going to help farmers all over this state—"

Slowly he turned his face. His eyes met hers. "Spare me."

"Farmers all over this state—" she said, trying to forge on.

He refused to let her. "I said, 'spare me.' I'm beginning to see why you're in advertising. You lie extremely well."

This time her anger didn't prickle, it flared through her like a small volley of fireworks. "I'm *not* a liar."

He gazed at the edge of the porch ceiling again. "Right," he nodded. He crossed his arms and closed his eyes again, shutting her out.

"I'm *not* a *liar,*" she insisted hotly. "And you haven't any right to call me one." When he paid no attention, she poked her finger against his shoulder. "And stop pretending to ignore me. If you're going to insult me, at least look me in the eye when you do it."

He looked at her. The expression in the hazel eyes was unfriendly in the extreme and shook her more than she cared to admit. She wished she hadn't touched him. It made electric prickles course through her body, as if she had stuck her finger in a light socket.

"Why," he asked with rancor, "should I look at you? I've seen what you've got to offer. Nice, but I'm trying to stay unimpressed. I'm tired. I've been messed with enough for one day. Don't keep adding temptation to my trials, all right?" To emphasize his point, he closed his eyes again. The set of his mouth indicated that he wanted only to be left alone.

Tess's jaw tightened. If she didn't need his cooperation on the calendar project, she would have been tempted to swear at him or hit him over the head with something. She confined herself to clenching her fist as hard as she could. "What's *that* mean? 'What I've got to offer?' I haven't offered you anything. *What* temptation?"

With a weary sigh he opened his eyes. He glanced pointedly at the flimsy robe. "You certainly seem to be offering. And I'll admit, it's tempting."

Her face grew hot with anger, and she put her hand to the front of her robe, pulling it more tightly shut. "Do you think I'm trying to seduce you?" she said in disbelief. "You, you conceited pig!"

"Steady," he said mildly, raising his hand in a signal to stop. "You've got to stay on my good side, remember? Calling me a pig is not conducive to staying on my good side. This time, I'll let it pass."

"I don't think you have any right to say that I *offered* you anything at all—"

He reached over and adjusted the collar of her robe. There was infinite contempt in the gesture. "You follow me out here in the moonlight, you're wearing this gauzy little thing, and you stand there with it falling open and your considerable charms on display—and they display very nicely by the way—oh, I think I have the right, all right."

He crossed his arms again. Frowning, he stared out at the horizon, ignoring her more pointedly than before.

Tess's face grew hotter still. Her cheeks felt as if they almost flamed. "Just because you're handsome, don't think you're irresistible."

He looked up, askance, at the star. "I don't think I'm irresistible. And I don't put much stock in looks. Sorry, but that's going to have to include yours."

"My looks aren't the issue here," Tess snapped back.

"They're actually very nice looks," he said, boredom in both his face and voice. "They really are. I admit that, for what it's worth." He yawned again.

"What's this obsession of yours with looks?"

"I'm not obsessed with them," he returned evenly. "I just don't like people who judge by them. They don't mean squat. Sorry."

"Just what are you getting at?" she asked, her eyes narrowing.

He shook his head as if disdainful that she couldn't tell. "That you should go inside. We'll pretend this never happened."

"Pretend *what* never happened?" Tess demanded with passion. "I didn't even know you were out here. You really are the most conceited man I ever—"

"Just go in," he repeated. His tone had the wary firmness that adults use with troublesome children. "It won't work. You won't use your—sexual allure—to cement the agreement. I gave my word I'd sign the release. You don't have to try to sweeten the deal to make sure I don't back out."

Tess tossed her head. She stood and glared at him, yanking the belt of the robe tighter. "Never in my life have I used sex to—"

With startling swiftness he, too, was on his feet. For a man so large, he moved with astonishing quickness. "I'll escort you inside. If you're not using sex, you gave the best imitation of it I ever saw. You're also trying to use me. In case you haven't noticed, I don't like it."

He locked one hand firmly around Tess's upper arm and tried to propel her toward the front door. She refused to budge. She tried to push his hand away and found she could not. He was too strong, and the hand burned into her flesh like a brand.

"Take your hand *off* me," she almost spat. "Nobody's using you. What *is* it that bothers you so much about letting us having your picture? Are you like one of those savages that thinks a photo steals his soul?"

"Oh, I can be a savage," he said, bending nearer. "As for what's wrong, I find the whole project demeaning, that's what. Pictures of me spread all over the state—me without a shirt, yet. Me on a calendar that purports to be of *hunks*, yet. Yesterday I was a respectable guy, minding my own business. Today my picture's in papers all over Nebraska, and I'm supposed to be a—a damned sex object or something."

Tess had despaired of prying his fingers from her arm. As she raised her face to him, she hoped he could see the sparks snapping in her eyes. "Poor you," she sneered and tossed her head.

He pulled her closer, the set of his mouth grimly angry. "It's not funny. I don't happen to like being viewed as an object."

"Strike up the violins," she said as sarcastically as she could. "Get out the handkerchiefs."

"I said it's not funny," he muttered between his teeth. "It's not easy to deal with."

Tess shrugged flippantly, although his moon-silvered face was truly angry. "I could deal with it. But then, I'm a mature, adult person."

"Really?" he asked, taking her by both arms and pulling her closer to him still. He lowered his face to hers, his mouth drawn down wrathfully at one corner. "Then try this."

His lips bore down on hers without an iota of tenderness. The mouth that captured hers was hot, relentless and demanding. The arms that held her were crushing, inescapable.

Tess's heart vaulted first in outrage, then in fear. There was no gentleness in this kiss, no affection, no respect. There was only hunger, naked and insistent.

When she tried to struggle, his arms tightened and he kissed her so hard that she bent beneath his force. She felt as if she were being ravished in both flesh and spirit.

When she managed to turn her face away, his kisses burned along the curve of her neck. "Stop," she ordered, her voice shaking. He did not stop.

"You're a mature, adult person," he said against her throat. "Deal with it." He seized her jaw between his thumb and forefinger and turned her face up to his so that he could kiss her again.

His hand slipped sinuously from her face to her throat to her shoulder, down her back and to her waist. He drew her to him so tightly that she gasped. When her lips parted, he used the opportunity to taste more deeply, more completely still.

Tess was alarmed, both by the force of his passion and her own complex response to it. Part of her reacted exactly as he wished, with humiliation and resentment. He was showing her what it was like to be used, and he was right—it was demeaning, wrong and shameful.

Yet part of her did not want his kiss to stop so much as she wanted it to change. It would be altogether different thing, she knew, to be held in his arms and given those things he took such pains to deny: love, tenderness, regard.

That they were missing made a strange ache surge through her body.

Tears rose in her eyes. He was treating her like an object. She hated it, and suddenly she hated him for doing it. With all the force of her being, she wished she had not come to this terrible place with its memories and dangers. She wanted to be home, in the safe and barren little apartment in the city. She sobbed against his mouth.

The hands that held her so inexorably suddenly stilled, although they gripped her just as hard. His body tensed. The mouth upon her own grew less insistent. He drew his lips away and stared down at her, his eyes cold and wary.

Her chin quivered slightly and she fought to keep it steady. One tear spilled over and trailed slowly down her cheek. She gave him a long look in which indignation mixed with sorrow. "You proved your point," she said, her voice deadly with bitterness. "Now let go of me."

His face, which seemed all silver and shadows in the moonlight, grew troubled. "You're crying."

"It's not you," she asserted, her expression rigid with control. "It's being in a place like this again." She nodded angrily to indicate the house, the farm, the countryside. "It brings back too many memories. It's not you. You could never make me cry. Why would I cry over you?" She injected a remarkable amount of disgust in the word *you*.

She tried to push him away, but he wouldn't allow it. He raised his hand and used his thumb to wipe the tear away. He shook his head. "I didn't mean—" he began, but he didn't finish the sentence. His jaw tautened, and a muscle jumped in it. He smoothed her tumbled hair back from her forehead. "I would never hurt a woman. Never. It's just that I'm half-crazy tonight with being tired. And you kept pushing me."

Tess looked away. She bit her lip. "Don't compound this fiasco by apologizing. You've really acted like a brute. Let's just leave it at that, shall we?'' Once more she tried to break free of him. Once more he held her fast.

"I'm not a brute."

She tossed her head. "Don't put it to a vote."

"Dammit," he said, "I'd watch it if I were you. If you weren't such a sassy little thing, this would never have happened in the first place."

"Oh," she retorted, sounded braver than she felt, "so now it's my fault. The big, superior male was forced to put me in my place. Maybe I should apologize to you."

"All I wanted," he breathed, his voice intense, "is to show you how things shouldn't be. If I were going to kiss you again, I wouldn't kiss you like that."

Warnings of danger coursed through her, making her go cold. She looked up at him questioningly, her senses in a chaotic whirl. She didn't trust herself to speak.

He stared down at her, his gaze unsettlingly steady. He touched her face again, gently but with something in his touch that made her nerves blaze with awareness.

"No," he said, drawing her closer. The moonlight spilled on them like magic. "I wouldn't do it like that. I'd do it like this."

And bending his face to hers, he kissed her again.

CHAPTER FIVE

TESS COULD NOT have been more surprised if he had swept her up to fly among the clouds of stars. Her soft lips parted beneath his boldly questing ones. The warm, clean scent of him seemed more appealing than any perfume.

The strength of his long body enfolded her. His chest was hard against her breasts, and his shirt was crisp, smelling of prairie sun and wind. When he shifted her more intimately into his embrace, his sleeve rustled slightly.

His mouth seemed planned to fit hers, his arms designed to hold her close. His very body seemed contrived and devised to join with hers. The perfection in the way he touched her almost dizzied her. She started to put her arms around his neck, partly to keep her balance, partly to keep him so unbalancingly near.

Designed, she thought, with a jolt. *Planned. Contrived. Devised.* This kiss was just as cold-blooded as the other one. His first embrace had been to punish her. This one, just as calculated, was to seduce. He was a man whose caresses were as programmed as a computer.

She drew back. He tried to recapture her lips, but she ducked her head, pushing ineffectually away from him.

"Stop it," she muttered, more embarrassed than before. "You cornfield Casanova."

"Why?" he asked, challenge in his voice. "You like it. I like it. It's what you had in mind, isn't it? Maybe it wasn't such a bad idea."

So, she thought, appalled, she was right. This time it was conquest, impure and simple, that was on his mind. And he was egocentric enough to keep on thinking that she had designs on him, as well.

"I never had anything in mind," she practically hissed. "I came out here because I couldn't sleep."

"Right," he nodded. "Worried that I wouldn't sign the releases? Why don't you kiss me again, just to ease your mind?"

She shook her head, furious. "All I wanted was to be alone. To—face some old demons. Instead, I find a new one—you."

He gave her a sardonic half smile. "What demons? The ones driving you on to—where is it—New York?"

"None of your blasted business. You're missing the point. The point is that you don't interest me."

He gave an eloquent shrug. He took her by the arms and steered her so that her back was against the wall of the porch. He released her but leaned with his hands on either side of her so that his arms blocked her escape. "Oh, I don't flatter myself that I interest you as a person. But as a means? That's another matter. Tell me, just what have I got to do with your getting to New York?"

Tess looked away angrily, her heart beating hard. She pulled the robe more securely around her. He was a stubborn, pig-headed man who had made up his stubborn, pig-headed mind about her, and nothing she could say would ever convince him otherwise. She wished a thunderbolt would sizzle him into nothingness, right here and now.

"Ah," he said, "not talking? Let's try another tack. Your demons. What have they got to do with the country? You get a kind of hectic, haunted look in your eyes every time you say the word *farm*. Why?"

She shot him a brief but telling glare then looked away again. "Men like you. That's what I don't like about farms."

"You don't even know what kind of man I am." His voice was low, scornful.

"I know all right," she said between her teeth. "The kind that gives orders, demands obedience—"

"That's not me," he said, still scornful. "In spite of what you think. That's not me at all." Then his voice softened, almost imperceptibly. "It sounds as if somebody hurt you. Did they?"

"What do you care?"

He was silent a moment. He dropped one arm, clearing her a path. "Right," he said, his mouth crooked. "What do I care? Go to bed, Miss Avery. Go, alas, alone."

"And you," she said with false sweetness, "can go to hell till it freezes over."

"With all the other demons?" he asked, raising one eyebrow.

"With all the other demons," she said and left him standing there.

He looked after her with amusement. But once she was inside and the house was silent again, his faint smile vanished.

He sighed harshly, crossed his arms and stared at the starstrewn sky. She was a troubling woman, troubling the way only smart women could be. Especially when they were beautiful. And the way she'd come stealing out into the moonlight, her robe open, her breasts gleaming like pearl...every curving line of her body outlined...what was a man supposed to think? He had kissed her the first time to teach her not to play games.

The second time, though, he had no such excuse. She'd looked lovely, and for a moment she'd almost convinced him she was innocent rather than conniving, and he'd been too tired to resist.

That was all, he told himself again. He'd been too tired to resist. Now he wished he had never touched her.

She had awakened demons of his own. He'd done things he hadn't meant to do. He had felt emotions he hadn't meant to feel.

Damn the moonlight, he thought unhappily and shook his head. For a few seconds it had knocked all common sense out of his head. Damn the moonlight.

THE JAGGED CRY of a rooster woke Tess, that and the scent of baking bread. The air pouring in through the curtains was as cool, lively and pure as a mountain stream.

She sat up with a shock of déjà vu, a feeling that she had fallen backward through time and had awakened in this same place in this same way before.

No, she thought, staring at the shafts of sunlight falling through the window onto the polished floor. She was in a strange place, not a familiar one, a place she should escape for her own peace of mind.

With a pang she remembered last night's scene on the porch with Cal Buchanon. She had been a fool to go out dressed that way. She should have fled inside as soon as she realized he was there. He had been tired, angry and all too ready to believe she had come after him for no good purpose.

Now her tumultuous emotions stirred a deep, primitive urge to escape both the man and the place he owned. But before she did, she intended to make sure he didn't sabotage her future. She wanted the signed release in her hand.

She dressed hurriedly, brushed out her auburn hair and carefully put on her makeup. She made her way to the kitchen where she found Edna but no sign of Cal. A sleepy

Bunny sat in the breakfast nook, yawning luxuriously and spreading jam on a piece of toast.

Edna was wrapping cooled cinnamon rolls in foil and putting them in the big freezer. She wore a faded checkered apron and had a smudge of flour on her cheek, but her beautiful crown of gray braids was immaculate.

Cal, Edna said, had been working so hard that she had talked him into taking the morning off. She had asked him to go to the pond and catch some perch for lunch. She wouldn't hear of Tess going after him until Tess had something to eat.

Edna made her sit in the breakfast nook across from Bunny, and insisted they both take heaping portions of fluffy scrambled eggs, homemade sausage, freshly baked bread and homegrown strawberries.

"Personally," Bunny said languidly, "I think you're smart to get him to sign the release. He's probably out there right now, trying to figure out how to weasel out of this."

"Bunny!" Edna said with disapproval. "That man's never broken his word in his life. You ought to be ashamed."

Bunny spooned a single strawberry into her mouth and savored it. "He doesn't like the idea of my having a career. He wants to run my whole life. He's trying to make me go to college. I don't want to."

Edna put a hand on her hip. She stared down at Bunny with a patience that seemed sorely tried. "He's *not* trying to run your life. He wants you to have at least a year of college, that's all."

Bunny poked her spoon into her dish and selected another perfect red berry. She contemplated it critically. "He wants me to study bookkeeping or beekeeping or some boring thing. He wants me to conform. He has trouble with a woman who's independent and thinks for herself. Miss Avery's seen that—haven't you?"

She slipped the berry into her mouth, at the same time giving Tess such a righteous, wide-eyed glance, that for a terrible moment Tess wondered if the girl had seen the dreadful incident on the front porch.

"Did you have to go to college?" Bunny prodded. "I mean, they can't teach you talent. Isn't talent more important than education?"

Tess shook her head, unwilling to become ensnared in a family argument. "They're both important. I—I wanted to go to college."

"See?" Bunny said, breaking off a tiny fragment of toast and studying it. "But I *don't*. People are different. If only *he'd* realize it." Daintily she ate the particle of toast. Then she stretched and stared out the window, as if lost in her own splendid dreams.

"Bunny," Edna said gently, "you'll understand better when you're older. He only wants what's best for you."

"Umm," Bunny said vaguely and kept staring out the window.

Edna sighed. She poured herself a cup of coffee and refilled Tess's cup as well. "I'll call the garage as soon as it opens and see if they can come out here," she said, changing the subject. "With luck, they can have your car going in no time. Although I saw Cal looking at it, and he didn't look a bit happy."

Tess smiled her thanks and studied the worry on the woman's handsome face. Edna, she thought, had her hands full with Bunny. Yet the girl, sitting there in the morning sunlight, seemed so full of spirit and dreams that Tess couldn't help but like her.

"I'd like to go find him and see if he'll sign that release," Tess said, folding her napkin and laying it beside her plate. "I brought new forms, but don't worry—you'll get full credit for the photo, Bunny."

Bunny turned to her, a happy, disbelieving smile on her lips. "You know," she said softly, "your accepting that picture—that's one of the greatest things that ever happened to me. And I guess maybe that you liking the picture enough to come clear up here to make sure you got it—even though Cal didn't want you to have it—is the other most wonderful thing that ever happened."

The pride and the gratitude on the girl's face was so touching that Tess didn't know what to say. As flippant and manipulative as Bunny might be, she obviously cared a great deal about her photography.

It was Edna who spoke. She put one arm around Bunny's slender shoulders. "Bunny," she murmured, "I hope someday you'll realize that one of the greatest things that ever happened to you was Cal."

Bunny, lost in her own happiness, didn't seem to hear.

THE POND was in an empty pasture beyond the big corral. Tess crossed the barnyard, watching ruefully as the dust settled on her white high-heeled toeless shoes. She nodded with controlled friendliness at two men working in the barn.

The bright sunshine spilled down. Somewhere, believing in the power of repetition, the rooster cried out again that it was morning. Tess inhaled deeply, and the scents in the air stirred a new storm of memory and emotion.

The sweet aroma of hay mingled with the warm, tangy one of horses and cattle. The dusty odor of grain mixed with the freshness of live grasses waving in the wind. Clover was in bloom, and its sweetness caressed the breeze.

I hate this, Tess thought, opening the pasture gate. *It's like being reminded of all the good things I've left behind, but none of the bad ones. It makes me want to be nostalgic when there's nothing worth being nostalgic about.*

The tall grasses tickled her ankles as she walked. Meadowlarks caroled. She set her teeth and kept striding toward a grove of elms and willows.

By the time she reached the pond, her hose were snagged and her shoes grass-stained. The pond had a shady side toward the house, and a sunny side toward the neighboring fields where horses and cattle grazed.

Cal stood on the sunny side, a fishing rod in his hand. He made an expert cast, and the line curved through the air.

Tess, feeling foolish and out of place in her city clothes, made her way toward him. She was sure he must have seen her coming, but he ignored her so completely she might as well have been invisible.

Did he still think she was some sort of clumsy, would-be seductress? It didn't matter what he thought, she told herself firmly and made her spine carry her even more straightly. Let him think what he wanted, as long as she got the job done.

He wore battered brown cowboy boots, tan jeans, and a yellow shirt, left half undone with the tail out. His hair shone almost blue-black in the morning light, and his skin gleamed like new bronze. The lines of his long body were a study in leisurely grace, but his gaze, fastened on the surface of the pond, was intensely concentrated.

The long-lashed hazel eyes stared at the red-and-white bobber floating on the water, and one dark brow was drawn studiously down. In the bright sunshine the straight nose and high cheekbones looked as regular as those of a Greek god, and the handsome mouth was set in absorbed attention.

Drat him, Tess thought irritably. There he stood, a conceited clodhopper by a country pond, his boots dusty and his shirttail out, yet still he was so handsome that it almost hurt to look at him. She reminded herself that he was just as arrogant and presumptuous as he was handsome—a feat one would have thought impossible.

She paused for a moment beneath the shade of a lone elm. She cleared her throat. He didn't look at her.

"I have to talk to you," she said. She adjusted an earring just to have something to do.

He reeled in his line, examined his bait and cast again. He still didn't look at her. "Talk," he said.

She squared her shoulders and closed the distance between them. She looked up at him, but the only sign that he was aware of her was the slight twitch of a muscle in his jaw.

"I'm going back to Omaha as soon as I can," she said between her teeth.

He nodded without emotion. "Good."

She opened her purse and pulled out the release form she had brought with her. "It'd make my job a lot easier if you'd sign this now. The matter would be over and done with."

He gave her a brief, sidelong glance. "Why should I want to make your job easier?"

She tossed her head in frustration. "Why do you enjoy making it *harder*?"

He watched as a dragonfly settled on the line. "You haven't exactly simplified my life, you know. Turnabout's fair play."

"Excuse me," she said. "But this isn't some scheme I hatched to torment you. I didn't come up with this calendar project. I didn't volunteer for it. I was assigned it. And it was *your* niece that sent in that picture and forged your signature. *I'm* an innocent bystander. The sooner you cooperate, the sooner I'm out of your way."

The muscle twitched in his jaw again. His expression was implacable. "I told you. I'll mail it in."

She rattled the paper. "Save yourself the price of a stamp. Look, my employer is very upset by this turn of events. If I can show her the release, she'll know the matter's resolved.''

He gave her another of his short, scathing looks. ''And you can get on with your brilliant career. Is that how it works? If you get high marks on this damned calendar project, you go up in the world?''

He sounded so contemptuous that Tess didn't care if he knew the truth. ''More or less. Why should you care?''

He shrugged, and his muscles did intricate things under the fabric of his shirt. ''I don't,'' he returned with a maximum of sarcasm. ''It just puts all your noble yap about farmers and ranchers and aid into perspective, that's all. The calendar's not going to do any real good, and you know it. You don't care.''

''I happen to care a great deal about the people in this state and their problems—''

''Then why are you leaving?''

Tess threw her hands out in a gesture of frustration. ''What difference does it make to you?''

''None,'' he replied evenly. ''I just like people to be honest. It's a quirk.''

She exhaled sharply, blowing a stray curl from her forehead. ''All right. Will you please sign this release so that I can get on with my 'brilliant career.' Then I'll be out of your life, and you'll be out of mine.''

He shrugged again. ''I said I'll send it. I won't be pressured. It's bad enough I agreed to be part of the fool thing. Don't push me any more. It's rude.''

''You're a great one to criticize, calling someone 'rude,''' she accused, putting a hand on her hip.

''Shh,'' he admonished. ''I've got a bite.''

The bobber flirted up and down in the water a few times, then went still. He swore beneath his breath. He obviously found the fish more important than he found her.

"You," she repeated, "are a great one to criticize *me* for being rude. After what you did to me last night—"

He turned to her. For the first time that day, she felt the full force of his dark eyes, and the displeasure in them was considerable. The yellow shirt made flecks of gold shine deep in their depths, like sparks.

"I'm sorry about last night," he said, but he sounded more angry than sorry. "Maybe I misread the situation. Maybe I didn't. Either way, it was unfortunate. I'd prefer to forget it. I hope you do, too. Under ordinary circumstances, I'd never have acted like that. You, unfortunately, have a gift for creating circumstances that aren't ordinary."

Tess looked up at him in amazement. "Is that supposed to be an apology?" she asked.

A dark lock of hair had fallen over his brow. He tossed it back impatiently. "Take it the way you want," he said, turning away from her again. "I suppose it is."

She glowered at him. Deliberately she reached out, grasped his fishing line, and tugged.

"Hey!"

"Do you know what this is?" she asked and tugged the line again, hard, so that the bobber danced.

His eyes met her flashing ones.

"I'll *tell* you what it is," she said. "It's a string with a worm on each end." She gave the line a third tug for good measure, then released it with a flippant motion.

Carefully and with great deliberation, he set the rod on the bank. He straightened and looked at her. The corner of his mouth skewed downward in annoyance. "Last night you called me a pig. This morning you call me a worm. I seem to be descending rapidly through the animal kingdom. Before you call me a dysentery amoeba, may I remind you that *you're* the one who wants a favor from *me*? You ought to watch that pretty mouth."

"No wonder you can't control your niece," Tess countered. "You're the most high-handed—"

"Leave my niece out of this," he ordered.

"High-handed, insensitive—*lout*. No wonder she's dying to get away from you."

The gold sparks in his eyes crackled more dangerously. Somewhere a meadowlark released a bolt of song, sounding incongruously cheerful.

"Leave Bunny out of it. You don't know anything about us." He flexed the fingers of his right hand, as if keeping tight control of himself.

They stared at each other for a charged moment. Although the sky was clear and a perfect blue, electricity seemed to shake the air between them.

"Go back to Omaha," he said at last. "Go back now."

She blinked in surprise, taken aback.

He reached into the pocket of his jeans. He drew out a ring of keys. "Take Bunny's car. She won't be using it. And yours won't be going anywhere for a while. I looked at it."

"What?" she asked, confused. "But the mechanic's coming—"

"He'll tell you the same thing I'm telling you," he said. "Take her car. But get out of here. Now. Before you do any more damage."

"Damage?" Tess asked in consternation. "What damage have I done? All I've tried to do—"

"I don't like the example you set for my niece for one thing. I don't like the way you keep trying to railroad me for another. And for a third, I don't like what you stand for, Miss Avery. Advertising tries to create an artificial world. It does it by twisting things. I like things real, and I like them honest. Consequently, I'm afraid I'd like you gone. Now."

Tess straightened, as if in reflex to a slap. She could only stare at him. His words hurt more than she could have thought possible. Her very soul stung. What right did he have to say such things?

He took her right hand, opened it palm up and dropped Bunny's car keys in it. "The white Mercury hatchback," he said, closing her fingers around the keys. He held her hand clenched shut so that she couldn't fling them back at him. "One of my men has a doctor's appointment in Omaha next week. I'll have him drop off your car and pick up Bunny's. Give your address to Edna."

He took his hand away. She opened her fingers and stared first at the keys, then up at him. "You can't give me her car—it isn't right—she'll be upset—"

He put a finger on her lips to quiet her. "The car's in my name. I decide what's right around here. I'll mail you the release. As I said I would. Now go. Edna may make you feel welcome. Bunny certainly will. But I'm not even going to pretend to try."

He took his finger away. He stared down at her for a long moment that they both found disturbing. For Tess's part, she felt wounded, angry and puzzled as well. What had she done to incur such hostility in the man?

Edna and Reverend Yonke both spoke glowingly of Cal's kindness. In the pictures, his elder niece, Marissa, looked at him with clear adoration. But Bunny painted him as an unreasonable tyrant, and Bunny, she thought, must be right. He was a man who could not tolerate a certain kind of woman. Her kind.

As for Cal, looking down into her brown eyes, he already regretted his harshness, but he could see no alternative. Last night the woman had brought out the worst in him. She had done so again this morning.

Stronger than any remorse he felt was his worry and anger over how she affected Bunny. Tess's presence had inspired Bunny to new heights or depths of cunning.

This morning when he'd looked at the woman's car, he'd felt half-sick. The water pump had been punctured as if by an ice pick. Bunny had done it, he was sure, to keep this glamorous creature around to put pressure on him.

Even before Bunny's latest descent into petty crime, the woman had made him edgy and resentful. She had disrupted his life with her fool calendar, she'd embarrassed him with the stupid newspaper story, and she was complicating his already troubled relationship with Bunny.

From the moment he'd seen her, he'd been on guard. He supposed that in the shadowy places of his mind, she reminded him of his sister, Bunny's mother. She had the same quickness of mind and spirit, the same neat, natural elegance, the same sense of style. To Bunny, Tess Avery probably looked like the most sophisticated creature on earth. And he didn't want Bunny thinking that—it was too dangerous. It was as though his sister Barbara were reaching from beyond the grave to put her claim on the girl once again.

He would not allow it to happen. He would protect Bunny, no matter how rude or crude he seemed to outsiders like this woman, or how much Bunny herself resented it.

Emotions flickered over the woman's face now. Her dark eyes flashed resentment, but her mouth quivered slightly, even as her chin rose defiantly higher. The breeze stirred her auburn hair, making her foolish black earrings swing lightly, ruffling her impractical white skirt.

Without wanting to, he remembered what it felt like to hold her in his arms, to feel her lips beneath his own. Only this time, he thought, there was no moonlight on which to blame such thoughts.

"Go back," he said, his face impassive.

Tess stood her ground. She intended to go, but not before she had her say. "My mother always told me, 'Handsome is as handsome does,'" she uttered, her voice cold.

"I'm glad that a calendar can only show the outer you. The inner one isn't very impressive."

She refolded the unsigned release and thrust it into his hand.

"But I'll give you some free advice," she said with a toss of her head. "You may love that girl, but you're going to drive her off. Trust me. I can see you as she does. Only if I were her, I'd already be long gone—from this place and from you. And I'd never look back."

She turned and walked away. She could feel his stare following her, drilling like a cold spear through her back.

Her high heel twisted on a hummock of grass, and her ankle almost twisted. Swearing silently, she stopped long enough to reach down and take off her stained shoes. Holding them in one hand and keeping her pleated skirt in place with the other, she strode across the pasture at a distance-eating pace.

Cal folded his arms and watched her go. *Good riddance,* he thought fiercely.

Her righteous words about Bunny rankled him to the core. She didn't know anything about the situation. She didn't know a particle of it. But she had managed to make things worse, far worse than anyone except himself knew. He and Bunny would clash over the business of sabotaging the car, and he knew they would clash badly.

Still, glad as he was to see Tess leave, something in her bearing touched him. At first, trying to make her way in the silly shoes, she had looked awkward and almost comical, yet proud, too.

But once her shoes were off, she moved with surprising economy and grace. She did not bother with the pasture gate this time, she simply pulled her skirt more tightly around her and slipped through the fence, between the strands of barbed wire. She did it as smoothly as the farm girl she claimed once to have been.

Past the fence, she didn't bother putting on her shoes again. She moved purposefully toward the house, every motion as natural as that of a leaf on the wind or a ripple in a stream. He realized there was much he didn't know about her, much that mystified him.

But he also realized, watching her walk away, what bothered him most about her. Like his sister years ago and like Bunny now, this woman could move in two different worlds.

Part of her was at home here, on the rolling plains of Nebraska, but another part belonged to a different life, a harsher, faster, more glittering one.

Women who could move in two different worlds, he knew from bitter experience, did not necessarily truly belong in either of them. They thought they knew what they needed. They thought they knew what they wanted. They even thought they knew what was important.

But such women never really knew. That was why they were so dangerous.

CHAPTER SIX

"I GOT STUCK in darkest Lawler County," Tess told Delia on the phone. She had been so anxious to escape from Cal's place that she had waited until she was on the road to phone the office. Now she stood in a filling station in the heart of the town of Lawler.

"I'm on my way back. I had to borrow a car. Mine has a hole in its whatsis-pan, and they have to send for a part. I'll have to stop home and change before I come in. But tell Mrs. Madigan the Buchanon man's agreed to let us use the picture."

"Did he sign a release?" Delia asked.

Tess winced, even though she had expected the question. "No. But he *swore* he'd mail it in. It was the best I could do."

"Can you really trust a man that handsome?"

A good question, Tess thought. "We haven't got much choice. I'm told he's a man of his word."

Delia laughed. "Obviously too good to be true. So how *is* his handsome hunkiness? Is he really that handsome? Is he really a hunk? Or is he five feet tall in real life?"

Tess ran her hand through her bangs. "He's handsome. I don't think he'd like the term *hunk*. He's about six foot three."

"Oh, *my*," said Delia, who was tall and liked tall men. "Well, something must be wrong with him, otherwise he can't be real. So what is it?"

"He only has one drawback," Tess replied. "He's a beast. Oh, and he hated me on sight. He reviled and insulted me and pretty well kicked me off his place."

"Well," Delia said philosophically, "nobody's perfect."

"Thanks," Tess muttered. "I'll see you in a couple of hours. Thurmond Spreckles is going to be a picnic after this."

The rolling countryside between Lawler and Omaha was afire with luxuriant shades of green. Tess had always loved the vividness of the summer fields and meadows, but today they had no power to soothe her.

She had returned to Cal's house to find a mechanic from town looking at her car engine and shaking his head. "Doesn't look good," he said mournfully. "No, ma'am, it just does not look good." He said he would have to tow the car in and send for a part. It would be a week at least before the motor was running again.

When he was gone, towing the car behind his truck, Tess, embarrassed, had to explain to Bunny and Edna that Cal wished her to be gone. She also had to tell them that he had told her to take Bunny's car.

"My car?" Bunny wailed. "He's letting you take *my car*? I hate him, I hate him, I hate him! I think he's giving me an ulcer—I really do!" She had dashed out of the room, clutching her stomach as if she were in agony.

Tess had never felt so odious, and never had she resented anyone as much as she did Cal Buchanon at that moment. But Edna insisted that if Cal said she was to take the car, then she was to take it without apology. Bunny would be fine, she assured her. The girl was emotional, that was all, and had a nervous stomach. Tess should not feel guilty.

What a mess, Tess thought, as she headed into the traffic of the interstate. She didn't want to imagine the latest clash between Bunny and Cal.

She felt sorry for the girl. Deep in the back of her mind, she felt sympathy for Cal as well. Bunny was as difficult as she was creative, and she had gotten Cal involved in something he obviously hated. He struck Tess as a serious man, possibly even a retiring one, who had no taste for such high jinks as the calendar project.

She shook such charitable thoughts from her mind. He was still horrible, she told herself. But when she remembered his kisses, she was filled with the strangest of sensations. *No,* she told herself. *Don't think of him touching you. Don't think of that at all.*

IT WAS almost noon when Tess finally arrived at the office. To cheer herself, she wore her best outfit, a pear-green linen suit and a plain scoop-necked white blouse.

Delia sat at the reception desk, looking cool and elegant in a white shirtwaist dress. But the expression on her face, as Tess walked in, was distinctly odd. It seemed to convey foreboding and reluctance.

Tess stopped and stared at her. Delia gave a delicate shrug and looked away, almost as if she were guilty. Tess understood immediately. Something was wrong.

"What is it?" Tess said, her voice flat with apprehension.

"Welcome back," Delia replied, then cleared her throat.

"Delia, I know that look on your face. Something's wrong. What?"

Delia put her elbows on her desk and folded her hands. "You're basically a rational, centered person who can handle a little crisis now and then. Aren't you?"

Tess eyed her warily. "It depends. What's the crisis?"

Delia studied her manicure. "Mrs. Madigan wants you to go back to Lawler."

"What?" Tess almost cried. "I just came from there."

Delia shook her head as though that were of no importance. "She wants you to go see the Buchanon man again."

"What?" Tess repeated with rising horror. "I'm still bleeding from the last time I saw him. Can't I lie in a cave and lick my wounds for a while? The man *hates* me, Delia. He hates *us*."

"Ah," said Delia, meeting her eyes at last. "The man may hate us, but women love the man. At least the editors at *Modern Woman* do. And they think the rest of the country will, too. They want to do a cover story on our calendar men."

Tess opened her mouth but couldn't seem to form a sentence. "*Modern Woman*?" she managed to say. It was the women's magazine with the largest circulation in the country.

Delia nodded. "The one and only. They called Mrs. Madigan this morning. She says the Buchanon man cinched it for them. They want to spotlight him in the story—full-page spread. You know what that means?"

Tess shook her head numbly. "It means he'll want to kill me. He hates the publicity he's already got. He will, Delia, he'll want me dead."

"Well, other than that little detail," Delia said, "it means this project gets the best possible national publicity. And that, girlfriend, sells calendars. And that's the name of the old advertising game."

Tess felt slightly sick. "But he'll have to agree to another complete set of releases. Good grief, we don't even have the first one in hand yet. If he hears this, he may pull out of the project altogether."

"Tess, you can't let him pull out," Delia said earnestly. "At this point, he *is* the project. You know what *Modern Woman* is willing to pay Homestead Heritage for this story? Twelve thousand dollars. That's a lot of help for this state. To say nothing of how many calendars it'll sell. Which means even more aid money. We won't just be a statewide project. This is national, now. This is big stuff. Mrs. Madigan is *very* excited."

Tess sat down weakly in one of the lobby's flowered easy chairs. "Can't I just phone him?" she asked. "I'd just as soon not look at him in the eye as he ruins my entire career."

"Hmm," Delia said firmly. "He's not answering his phone again. Somebody has got to go talk to him. Now. An article in *Modern Woman*? This is good for another press release."

Tess rested her elbow on the arm of the chair and leaned her forehead on her hand. "I suppose if I don't get him to say yes, I can kiss any recommendation for New York goodbye. I can probably kiss my job goodbye, too."

Delia gave her a sympathetic look. "She didn't actually put it into so many words."

"No," Tess said miserably. "She put it into one of those *looks* of hers. You know, one of those Do-It-or-Die-Trying looks."

"Well, yes," Delia admitted, her voice unhappy. "She did have that look, now that you mention it. You know how she is when she really wants something. The Dragon Lady."

Damn! thought Tess and rubbed her eyes tiredly.

"When does she want me to go?" she asked at last.

"Now would be fine," Delia said. "An hour ago would have been even better."

Tess, her hand still over her eyes, shook her head. What in heaven's name, she wondered, was she going to say to Cal Buchanon about this latest development? Would he even talk to her at all?

"Hey," Delia said brightly. "Remember what Madigan always says. Don't look on this as a problem. Look on it as a challenge."

Tess gave her exactly the sort of look she deserved.

"WHAT ARE YOU doing back?" Bunny asked, wide-eyed with amazement. "Is your car fixed? Did you bring mine back? I nearly died when Cal made you take it."

Bunny had been on the front lawn, brushing the collie when Tess drove up. She had run to the car immediately.

Shaking her head, Tess got out of the car. "Bunny—I'm sorry about your car. I didn't have much choice except to take it. I need to talk to your uncle. Where is he?"

Automatically Tess began to head for the house. Bunny tugged at her arm, begging her to stop. The girl wore shorts, a baggy blue T-shirt, no shoes and no makeup. Tall as she was, she looked younger than her seventeen years. Alarm washed over her face. "Something's gone wrong. About the picture. Hasn't it?"

Bunny's expression was so filled with fear and disappointment that Tess patted her hand. She looked around apprehensively for any sign of Cal. "No. Nothing's gone wrong. Something's gone very right, in fact. But I have to get him to sign a more extensive release. If he'll do it."

Bunny kept hanging on to Tess's elbow. Her expression changed to one of excited puzzlement. "What? Why? What's happened?"

Tess realized she had said more than she should, and she hoped Bunny would settle for a vague answer. "We have a chance for some national coverage," Tess murmured. "But I have to talk to him."

She started to move toward the house, but Bunny held her back. "He isn't there. Neither is Edna. Cal's in the barn. Edna's in town. National coverage? What kind? Newspaper? Magazine? You mean my picture could be printed in papers all over the country?"

Bunny was getting so excited that she almost danced as she clung to Tess. "You mean a picture that I took could be going out over the A.P. wires? It could be in *The New York Times* and everyplace?"

"Bunny," Tess said, "settle down. It's an inquiry from a magazine, that's all."

"A magazine?" Bunny cried, even more excited. "What magazine?"

"A women's magazine."

"What women's magazine? Which one? A big one?"

"Bunny," Tess almost pleaded, prying the girl's fingers from her arm, "please. I can't tell you any more. I just can't. I have to talk to your uncle. He's in the barn? Is his mood any better?"

"His mood is *terrible*," Bunny said. "As usual. A magazine! I can't believe this! I'm going to call Fred—he'll be so proud. He's always told me I could make the big time. Oh, this is a dream come true."

The girl sprang away and ran into the house, so excited that the dog followed her, barking in perplexity. Bunny, slamming barefooted into the house, displayed all the maturity and dignity of a six-year-old.

Now, what have I done? Tess wondered, gritting her teeth. She hoisted her white shoulder bag higher and headed for the barn. Dust was about to ruin the polish of another pair of white shoes, but that was the least of her worries.

The barn had the sweet hay and animal scent that Tess had known from childhood. Shadows hung in its cavernous space, softening the building's angles, and where sunlight fell through the open doors, dust motes danced in the rays.

She narrowed her eyes, searching the barn's dim recesses for Cal. At last she saw him. He was in a stall, kneeling beside a big dappled-gray quarter horse. He was winding a bandage around the horse's foreleg.

She stood silhouetted in the sunlight slanting through the barn door. Straw crackled beneath her high heels. She cleared her throat. "Mr. Buchanon? It's me—Tess Avery. I hate to bother you again, but something's come up."

She saw how still he suddenly went. He looked up slowly. His eyes met hers.

"You," he said between his teeth. He wasn't happy to see her. He was still seething from the scene Bunny had made this morning when he'd confronted her about Tess's car. All this woman meant was trouble.

He set down the horse's hoof and stood. He still wore the yellow shirt, completely unbuttoned now. Wisps of straw clung to it, and it was streaked with perspiration from the afternoon heat.

Keeping his eyes on her, he swiftly buttoned the shirt and tucked it in. "I thought you went back to Omaha." His low voice was almost a growl.

She fingered the lapel of her green jacket nervously. "I did. They sent me back. There's a new development. May we talk?"

Disgust etched his face. "What have I done to deserve this?" He looked around his barn, as if someone might appear with a reasonable answer. "All I want is to live my life and raise that kid in peace."

Tess took several steps toward him. He looked down with distaste at her high-heeled white shoes, then scanned her body in the elegant outlines of the suit. "Do you always dress like this to visit a barn?"

"I didn't know I was coming to a barn," she said, stopping before him. "If you'd answer your phone, I wouldn't have had to come back at all."

She reached out automatically and scratched the gray behind its ears. The horse bumped her hand playfully and nuzzled her sleeve with its velvety lips.

Cal watched her for a moment, a dubious downward quirk to his mouth. Then he took her by the arm and led her away from the gray, closing the door of the stall. "Come on. If my horse eats your jacket, I'm not going to pay for it."

He had led her to a neat stack of hay bales almost as tall as he was. He released her arm with the same impersonal quickness he had taken it. "What is it now?"

Tess tossed her head nervously and straightened her jacket again. Even though he stood an acceptable distance from her, he seemed too close. And although his touch on her arm had been anything but friendly, the spot where his hand had gripped her burned with a surprising warmth.

All the way back to Lawler County she had rehearsed how she would break this latest piece of news. She had planned it, down to when to pause and when to take a breath. She had revised and improved her speech until only a heartless ogre could refuse her and say no.

"No," Cal said when she finished. As her story had unfolded, his handsome face had at first looked disbelieving, then appalled, then so expressionless it might have been carved of stone.

With rising panic Tess watched his features harden. And, she noted with alarm, that if his face showed no emotion, his body language bespoke volumes of it, all dangerous. He seemed somehow taller to her, the width of his shoulders menacing. His hands hung at his sides as tensely as a gunfighter getting ready to draw.

She swallowed hard. "Now listen again to the advantages—please. It's twelve thousand dollars instant profit to the Homestead Heritage Foundation. Plus the publicity will probably boost calendar sales by the thousands—maybe the tens of thousands. You *can't* say no."

"No," Cal said. Deep in his long-lashed eyes she could see the gold flecks starting to burn.

"But you can't—"

He cut her off with a disgusted gesture. "No. I'm not going to have my picture smeared all over some silly magazine. No. I'd look like an idiot. Sandwiched between girdle ads and cookie recipes? No way. Get yourself another man."

"I can't get myself another man," she said desperately. "They want you. You're the one they're excited about."

He made the same brusque gesture of lost patience, his face dark with anger. "No. Some men like having their pictures taken. I don't. And if it gets taken, it's for the family, not a bunch of people I don't even know. Especially women-people. No."

"Listen," Tess implored, "I'm not saying this to flatter you, but you're a—a handsome man. Very handsome. It's your photo that makes the magazine want to pay that kind of money."

He swore, shaking his head. "What difference does it make what I look like? Why do people care what anybody looks like?"

"But that's the whole *point*," Tess argued. "The calendar is supposed to be pictures of good-looking men."

"Why don't you make it of good-looking women instead? Be in it yourself, if you think it's such a great idea— I've had a bellyful of people fussing about 'good-looking.' I'm sick of it. Leave me in peace, will you?"

"What do you mean?" Tess asked, staring at him in dismay. "What do you mean you're sick of it?"

He leaned a fraction of an inch closer. "I mean just that—sick. I'm a human being, not a show horse or something. If I've got any value it's for what I've done with my ranch and my family and my community. Not, for God's sake, what I *look* like."

Tess looked at him with a sinking feeling. She had a sudden intuition so strong that it shocked her into temporary numbness. He wasn't a conceited man. He was a modest one with a highly developed sense of privacy. Probably all his life strangers had judged him by his looks and not his character. Only a superficial man would like superficial judgments to be made about him. No wonder he had fought the idea of having his photo used.

"Look," she said, trying to marshal her best arguments. "I know how you feel about this, but it's for such a good cause—for an excellent cause. You have to think it over. You have to."

His mouth thinned, its line becoming close to threatening. "I don't *have* to do anything. Except run this ranch and take care of my family. And if you'll leave, I'll do just that. The answer, in case you missed it, Miss Avery, is *no*. Now leave. Don't ask any more of me. I've agreed to too much already."

She raked her hand through her bangs. She bit her lip. "Do you want me to beg?" she asked, hating herself as she said it. "All right. I'll beg. Please? Not just for the farmers and ranchers in this state, but for me? I know you don't like me, but look on the bright side. If you say yes, I'll be out of your life forever. I'll go far away. You'll never have to see me again. Please. *Please*."

"No," he said. "I'm not going to have my picture stuck between an article on Can This Marriage Be Saved and Be Creative with Cheese. I am not, I do not and will not consent to be called a—what's that god-awful word you used?"

"Hunk," Tess muttered miserably. "They want to call it Nebraska Hunks."

"Hunks," he said with loathing, then swore. He leaned his elbow on the top bale of the stacked hay. "Hunks," he repeated and swore again.

Tess closed her eyes as if in prayer. "I'm willing to do almost anything—anything to get you to agree," she said. Then her eyes snapped open, and she looked up at him in horror.

Why, she thought wildly, *did I have to say that, of all things?*

The look he gave her was coldly measuring. The black brows lowered in a disapproving frown. His body seemed even more taut and coiled with restless energy than before.

"I didn't mean that the way it sounded," she amended hastily. She shook her head in confusion. "I meant anything within reason—I meant we, as an agency, will negotiate with you to the best of our power—"

"I know what you meant." The scorn in his voice had the cold, scathing burn of ice. Once more he looked her up and down. This time his dark eyes seemed to strip the suit from her body, to examine her like a piece of property.

"No," Tess protested and bit her lip again. "I didn't mean *that*. It's just an expression—"

He nodded, a brief motion that managed to express considerable contempt. "I'm glad you said it. I was actually feeling bad about last night. Afraid I'd misjudged you. I even wanted to believe I'd misjudged you." He sighed roughly.

The look he gave her made her heart leap painfully. He leaned closer still, his face filling her vision. His beautiful eyes were full of anger. "Do you know what? I wanted to be wrong about you. I don't even know why. I even thought of coming after you, apologizing, saying, 'Look, this has been unfortunate. Let's start over.'"

His eyes held hers for a long moment, and she could not find her voice. *I'm not what you think,* she wanted to cry. *Why do you want, so much, to think the worst of me?*

He gave the bale of hay a dismissive slap. "But I wasn't wrong. So I'm glad I saved myself the disappointment. Well, is this the right place for a roll in the hay? You're not dressed for it, but we could take care of that in short order."

"I most certainly was *not* inviting you for a roll in the hay," Tess managed to object. "I wasn't." As overwhelmed by embarrassment as she was, she felt a hot prickle of anger stirring deep within her.

He raised his chin so that the look he cast her was even more disdainful. "You didn't have the nerve to go through with it last night," he said. "You just flirted with it. But today the situation's more critical. Stop looking like the picture of outraged innocence. Last night you came chasing after me in your nightgown. Today you make the offer outright. Thanks, but no thanks."

Her face blazed with resentment. "I didn't chase you. I didn't make you any offer. I just said something off the top of my head—"

He cut her off with a bitter smile. "But hardly from the bottom of your heart. And we both know why it got said—blind ambition. No, Miss Avery. You'll have to find another way to New York. I'm not a hunk, and I'm not your ticket out of here."

Tess's emotions swirled so wildly that her head throbbed and she thought she saw sparks of light falling through the air. A clutching sensation in her chest made her wonder if she was going to collapse. Not only was this man ruining her future, he was insulting her as he did so.

She made one last desperate attack, all her pulses pounding. She knew what she was about to do was unfair, but she saw no alternative. "You have to do it—for Bunny," she said in a choked voice. "You'll break her heart if you say no. She'll never forgive you. You know she won't."

His hand, which had been toying with a wisp of hay, went suddenly motionless. He stared down at her, and a vein jumped in his temple. His eyes narrowed like those of a man setting his sights on prey.

"You've already told this to Bunny?" His voice was ominously quiet.

Tess knew she had made another tactical error, a major one. "She'd find out anyway." That was true, she told herself nervously. Of course it was true. Bunny would have found out eventually. Wouldn't she?

He straightened to his full height. He made a restless, somehow threatening movement with his shoulders. His face had taken on the stone-like coldness that had shaken her so badly before. He reached for her.

Tess was too rattled to move away. His hand closed so tightly on her shoulder that it hurt. He took a step closer to her, his lip curling. "You don't stop at anything, do you?"

She looked at him numbly. The hand that gripped her shoulder tightened so much harder that she took in her breath. "Don't touch me," she said from between her teeth and cursed herself because her voice shook.

"I thought you'd let me touch you all I wanted to," he jeered. Roughly he pulled her to him. Tess gasped as he lowered his face nearer to hers. His lips almost touched her mouth.

"Stop it," Tess hissed, then inhaled sharply in apprehension. The scents of hay and sun-bronzed flesh filled her nostrils. He smiled at her, but his eyes were cold.

Using all her strength, she tried to push him away, but he was immovable. He pinned her against the bales of hay.

His face descended a fraction of an inch closer to hers. There was anger in his expression, and infinite disdain. His voice was low, both intimate and insolent. "I think you'd let me, all right." He nodded. "Touch you all I want. And to be honest, I want to. Don't ask me why. But I won't. The price is too high."

"Stop it," Tess repeated, more vehemently than before.

"It's stopped." His hands fell away, and he took a step backward. The hay rustled around his boots. He smiled at her again, the same indifferent, condescending smile. He reached out and took a piece of straw from the lapel of her green jacket. He flicked it away. It was as if he were flicking away the last shred of his regard for her.

"Leave, Miss Avery. Don't come back again. Or I won't sign any release at all." He turned his back and walked out of the barn.

Tess stared after his tall figure, her face hot. She leaned against the hay, her heart hammering. She closed her eyes. Things had gone worse than she could have imagined.

She turned and laid her forehead against the prickly hay, inhaled its comforting scent. The worst part, she knew, was that much of what had happened was her own fault.

She never should have told Bunny about the magazine. Cal had every right to resent her for doing that. Yet at the time, it seemed to have happened innocently enough. She had been confused and anxious, thinking more of Cal and her problem than of the girl. And Bunny had been insistent.

But then, foolishly, she had tried to use Bunny to play on Cal's emotions. She should have known he wouldn't tolerate such a thing. She should have known how it would anger him.

Her head pounded. She tried to force herself to breathe more slowly. Then she remembered her foolish words to him, and her head pounded harder. She clenched her fist and struck ineffectually at the hay.

I'm willing to do almost anything—anything to get you to agree. The words seared into her memory. What a stupid, stupid, stupid thing to say. Especially after last night. It had confirmed his least-charitable suspicions about her. She didn't even know why she had said it, except that it was the desperate kind of thing people say just before they give up hope.

Her face still hidden in shame and frustration, she hit the bale again as hard as she could. Cal thought she was a terrible person, meddling and ruthless. He thought she was unspeakably cheap. And it was her own fault. Stupid, stupid, stupid.

She straightened and wiped her hands across her heated cheeks. Turning, she glanced out the door. The barnyard seemed quiet, deserted. Cal must be inside the house now, she thought. Brushing at her suit jacket, she tried to adjust it back to its usual immaculate fit.

Head down, she left the barn and walked as quickly as she could to Bunny's car. She didn't want to take it again, but she had to escape from this place, and there was no other way.

She drove almost half a hundred miles before she felt even close to normal again. At first all she could think about was how completely Cal Buchanon must despise her.

As rationality returned, she realized with a sickening feeling how displeased Mrs. Madigan would be with her failure. Mrs. Madigan was not a woman who suffered frustration with grace. There would be recriminations. There would be consequences.

The first of these consequences would be that Mrs. Madigan wouldn't recommend her for the New York job. The thought left Tess feeling hollow and small.

Then a darker thought entered her mind, an ominous goblin of a thought. She had done things today that she normally would never do. Although Cal had told her not to intrude in his life anymore, she had gone back to his house to do just that. For her own welfare, she had tried to convince him to do something he obviously hated. She had even tried emotional blackmail on him, by playing on his troubles with Bunny. And, unwittingly, by telling Bunny about the magazine, she had most certainly made those problems worse.

Lastly, she had said that unforgivable thing. *I'll do anything to get you to agree.* She was not the sort to say that to a man. She would never do things that she knew were wrong just because they would further her career. She was not that kind of woman.

No? asked the goblin squatting in her brain. He grinned. In order to get to New York, she had done all those things. She had intruded, meddled, used every high-pressure technique she knew. She had tried to play on Cal's most private emotions, and she had set family member against family member.

She wasn't the type of woman to do anything to get what she wanted. But maybe that was the kind of woman she was becoming.

CHAPTER SEVEN

CLAIRE MADIGAN was a small, round woman who wore elegant suits and whose silver hair was always drawn back in the most impeccable of chignons. One of her enemies—and she was a woman powerful enough to have several—once said she resembled a perfectly groomed dumpling. Inside that soft exterior, however, was a heart and spine of stainless steel.

Mrs. Madigan sat at her French provincial desk, toying with an antique letter opener made of sterling silver. Her cool gray eyes met Tess's uneasy dark ones. "So his answer is no, is it?"

Tess nodded. She had spent a sleepless night anticipating this meeting. Any guilt she had felt about interfering with Cal Buchanon's life had fled. In its place was a sick conviction that she probably hadn't interfered and meddled nearly enough.

"So," Mrs. Madigan almost cooed. "So-o-o."

Tess studied her fingers laced together tensely in her lap. "Buchanon seems to have some very strong—feelings about this sort of thing. I don't think we should push him any farther. I'd hate to see him back out of the project altogether. He threatened to."

"Threats," mused Mrs. Madigan. She contemplated the glitter of the morning sunlight on the silver blade of the letter opener. "Well, as someone said, it isn't over until it's over. He may come around. I hope so for Homestead's sake.

I hope so for mine. I most especially hope so for your sake, Tess. Up until now you've seemed very—promising."

Up until now, Tess thought, her spirits plunging even lower. The room filled with silence, but the silence spoke to her, telling her she had failed and, in consequence, stood to lose everything.

Mrs. Madigan held the letter opener delicately at both ends and turned it slowly. "I've been in this game for a long time," she said at last. "A long, long time. There's an old saying—a chain is as strong as its weakest link. I perceive a weak link in this chain of circumstances. The niece. That's where you have to attack. Oh, subtly, of course. Obliquely, even. But that's the spot. You'll have to get at him through the niece."

Tess stiffened in apprehension. "I can't. Nothing would offend him more."

"But nothing else, my dear, will move him," Mrs. Madigan said, laying down the letter opener. She put her elbows on the desk and tented her hands together, looking over them at Tess.

"I—that—it wouldn't be fair," Tess said. The statement sounded weak and childish in her ears.

"It's for an *excellent* cause," Mrs. Madigan said calmly. "The end justifies the means. I'm not going to see this project torpedoed by some man just because he's having a fit of misguided modesty. I won't stand by and let it happen. And neither, my dear, must you."

Tess's muscles were so tense that her neck hurt. She could almost feel a noose tightening around it. She could not bear to interfere in Cal Buchanon's life again, she could not.

Mrs. Madigan smiled a smile of perfect sweetness. "It may sound hard to you, Tess. And I know that some people say that I'm a hard woman. I'm not. I'm merely determined. I love this state. I want to help it. I want this project to be the best of its kind ever done. And we can do it."

Tess squeezed her hands together more forcefully in her lap. She nodded her agreement because it was simpler than trying to put her complex feelings into words.

Mrs. Madigan's smile stayed in place. "Give him a few days to cool down. Then get to work on him. The niece is the key, as I say. You can figure out how to do it. A press release to her county's papers, perhaps. Local Girl to Get Photo Credit in National Magazine. Something like that. That would bring an uncomfortable amount of pressure to bear on him."

Tess said nothing. *I can't do that,* she thought.

"I know you can do it," Mrs. Madigan said. There was a significant pause. "At least," she said, smoothing her flawless hair, "I *hope* you can."

Her smile faded, and she gave Tess The Look. *Succeed or die,* said The Look. *Succeed or die. Failure will not be tolerated. Is that clear?*

For the third time Tess nodded. It was clear.

FOUR DAYS passed, and mercifully the weekend came. Tess had done nothing about Cal Buchanon.

On Saturday night she brooded alone in her small upstairs apartment on North 43rd Street. Delia had asked her to go to the Community Playhouse to see a production of *Macbeth,* but Tess begged off. The last thing she needed to see was a play about the evils of ambition. Besides, she knew that tonight she had to make her decision. She could postpone it no longer.

Her desk was battered and secondhand. So was her electric typewriter. She sat before it, barefoot, in blue jeans and an old University of Nebraska sweatshirt whose bright red had long ago faded to dullness..

Her chin in her hand, she stared at the press release she had just written.

FOR IMMEDIATE RELEASE

"*Modern Woman* magazine seeks to publish the work of local photographer, Barbara Jean Sevrinson, seventeen, a resident of Lawler County.

Sevrinson's photograph of her uncle, Lawler County rancher Cal Buchanon, was accepted by the Heritage Homestead Foundation Calendar Project earlier this month. Sevrinson is a senior at Lawler High School.

Modern Woman expressed interest in giving Sevrinson's work national exposure and in helping the Heritage Foundation to publicize the calendar.

"It's a singular honor for one so young as Barbara Sevrinson," said advertising executive Claire Madigan. "And it's a simply wonderful way to publicize the calendar and help our fellow Nebraskans."

Proceeds from the calendar will go to aid farmers and ranchers across the state.

It wasn't exactly poetry, Tess thought wanly, but it ought to do the job.

Once this was published in Lawler and the neighboring towns, how could Cal refuse to sign the release? He would embarrass Bunny in front of the entire county. He would seem like an insensitive lout destroying a young girl's dream. He would also seem like an uncharitable grump, unconcerned about the welfare of those farmers and ranchers less fortunate than he.

Yes, she thought again, a sick feeling in the pit of her stomach, that should do the job, all right.

Then she put her head in her hands. *I can't do this,* she thought. *I just can't.*

She squeezed her eyes shut. The image of Mrs. Madigan's cool smile hovered in her mind like that of the Cheshire Cat. Her equally cool words echoed. "I know you can do it. At least I *hope* you can."

"I can't do it," she muttered out loud. The blood pounded in her temples.

If she didn't do it, she could kiss the recommendation for the job in New York goodbye. It would be as if a door, tauntingly open and inviting, were slammed in her face and locked again, for who knew how long?

Worse, Mrs. Madigan's opinion of her would change. Tess would no longer be the bright newcomer with promise. She would be the one who wasn't working out. The one who didn't quite have what it took. The one who would have to be replaced.

"Damn!" said Tess aloud.

She straightened with a sigh. It didn't matter. She couldn't do it to Cal. And she couldn't do it to herself. She ripped the paper out of the typewriter, tore it into pieces and threw them into her dented wastebasket.

So I'll end up being fired, she thought. So what? It wasn't the end of the world. So what if she still had school debts? At least she knew her way around this part of the country. Her experience counted for something around here. There were other jobs. She'd get one and save her money, and she'd get to New York on her own. Eventually.

Eventually, she thought, half numb, half sick. Maybe it would take another year, maybe two. But someday she'd be debt-free and ready to take the plunge alone, without anybody's help. She pushed away from the desk and picked up the classified ad section of the *Omaha World-Herald*.

It was better to do something, anything, than just to think about how she was going to fail. If she was going to lose her job, then she would have to find a new one. She might as well start now.

The pages of the newspaper rattled as she scanned through them. Mechanically she scribbled down a few likely listings.

A struggling young ad agency wanted a copywriter. A complex of stores in the Benson area wanted a general manager with marketing experience. Two of the state colleges wanted business teachers. One was the college at Lawler.

She took her list and sat down at the typewriter again. Better to apply for a new job than sell her soul for the old one, she told herself.

But New York, she told herself. *I could have gone to New York—this summer.* The loss of the opportunity hurt, dealt her an actual physical pain. She forced herself to ignore it.

She typed up four brief letters of application. From her file cabinet she took a sheaf of résumés. They listed her educational credentials, her employment history, the projects she had worked on at the Madigan Agency, her references. She had a stack of them because that was often how she spent her evenings, trying to come up with the perfect résumé for the New York job.

She put the letters and résumés into envelopes, addressed and stamped them. Then she sat staring at them.

New York, she thought again with a pang.

Don't think about it, she warned herself. *Do something. Do anything.*

She put on her tennis shoes and went down the outside stairs of her apartment and got into Bunny's car. She drove up to North 45th Street and mailed the envelopes. They made a hollow, rattling *clunk* when she dropped them in the box.

Then she simply drove around aimlessly for an hour or two. She was not soothed.

At last she felt guilty for putting unnecessary miles on Bunny's car and headed back to 43rd Street. She parked the car in the driveway next to her landlord's vehicle and ran up the outside stairs to her apartment.

Just as she closed the door behind her, she heard another car pull into the drive. Her landlord's sister, she thought. The woman frequently came over on Saturday nights to play gin rummy with her brother.

Tess turned on a table lamp but didn't bother with the overhead. It didn't seem to her like a night for the glare of bright lights. The more muted and dim the world stayed, the better.

She kicked off her shoes and sat on her old couch, drawing her feet up under her. She put her head in her hands again and wondered if she ought to allow herself the luxury of a good cry.

An impatient knock at her door jolted her out of her unhappy reverie. Who could it be, she wondered, rising and going to the door to unbolt it. Her landlord? What would he want? Perhaps his temperamental refrigerator was rebelling again and he had come to ask for ice cubes.

She swung the door open, expecting to see her landlord's moonlike face. Instead she saw a man's chest. It was a broad chest, and its muscularity was apparent even under the pale buttoned-down shirt that clothed it.

Startled, Tess raised her eyes. Her gaze met the cool dark one of Cal Buchanon. The waning moon washed him with silvery light and made shadows play in the angles of his face. She took in her breath sharply and caught the scent of after-shave, an autumnal grassy smell mixed with something warm and leathery.

"Oh," was all she could say. She had forgotten how handsome he was. The sight of him stunned her a bit.

"My car," she managed to say. "You brought my car back."

He kept staring down at her but didn't say a word. The warm night breeze stirred the blackness of his hair. He nodded.

Tess tried to get her breath. It had deserted her. "And you want Bunny's keys. I'll get them. And a check for gas and repairs."

"I want to come in," he said without smiling. "I want to talk to you."

She shrugged casually, but her heart pumped wildly against her ribs. "Of course."

She stepped back and let him enter. He wore black slacks and a shirt that was either white or pale blue. She couldn't tell in the dim light. He wore a tie, and that surprised her, although he looked fine in it. As if to offset the formality, his sleeves were rolled halfway to reveal his powerful forearms. He was one of those rare men whom dress clothes made him look more masculine than ever.

He shouldn't be allowed to dress up, Tess thought, shaken. He looked too good. Some poor woman would see him and fall over dead from pleasure.

The pale shirt made his hair look blacker than ever, his eyes darker, his tan deeper. Its tailored lines emphasized the regularity of his features and the width of his shoulders.

"May I sit?" he asked. There was a tone in his voice that she couldn't identify. Was it boredom? Resignation? Dislike?

"Certainly," she said. She stood, her hands clasped together and pressed against her waist. She was embarrassed that her feet were bare, her jeans were old and that she wore no makeup.

He sat on the old green couch. He crossed his legs, his right ankle on his left knee, and leaned one arm on the back of the couch. Although it was a casual position, he seemed full of restless energy. His gaze roamed the dimly lit apartment, taking in its bareness. Its only ornaments were Tess's beloved posters.

His eyes returned to her, looked her up and down, from the top of her windswept hair to her bare feet. At last they settled on her face. "This is a hard place to find. I didn't expect you'd live like this. This neighborhood's kind of rough, isn't it?"

Tess shrugged self-consciously. She sat down on the arm of the overstuffed chair. "The rent's low. It's close to the bus lines in case my car breaks down."

At the mention of her car, he grimaced slightly. Then he went back to his unsettling study of her face, his own unreadable. "That's another thing. Your car. It sounds like a cheap party noisemaker. You should get a better one."

She shrugged again, although she knew the car had become such a rattletrap it was probably dangerous. "It'll have to do," she said as if it didn't matter. In truth she worried about the car constantly.

He glanced around her apartment again. "You don't dress like somebody who lives like this." His gaze flicked over her jeans, sweatshirt and bare feet. "Not usually, anyway."

She raised her chin slightly. "I have to have clothes for work. I'm supposed to represent a successful business."

"I see." He gave a sardonic nod. "So all your money goes on your back. You ought to save a little out. Buy yourself some light bulbs."

Tess didn't know what to say, so she stuck her feet out and concentrated on wiggling her toes. She stopped when she realized Cal was watching her more closely than before. She drew her feet back in and crossed her arms, almost hugging herself. "Look, can I make you some coffee or something? What is it exactly that I can do for you?"

He ignored her offer of coffee. He took a deep breath, then exhaled it. He gave every appearance of a man about to do something he hated. "I changed my mind," he said at last. "I'll sign your damned releases for the magazine."

Tess's lips parted in surprise. Still hugging herself, she stared at him. The muscles of his jaw were tense, his mouth turned down, and distaste mingled with resignation in his expression.

You just saved my life, Tess thought. Relief flooded through her in a sweet, intoxicating wave. "You will?" she asked in happy disbelief.

He raised one dark brow in dismissive scorn. "I will."

She slid down into the seat of the chair, never taking her eyes from him. Her legs were still draped over the arm, but she gave no thought to how undignified the position was. "Why?" she demanded, too relieved and curious to be polite.

He stood, jamming his hands deep into his pockets. He began to pace the small living room restlessly. "A man has choices," he muttered. "He has to decide what's important. What's best for the people he—what's best for his family."

He turned and looked down at her. The grimness of that look made her hug herself harder than before. "What would have been best is if you'd never shown up at all. But you did. Like a beautiful young devil. Your hands full of temptations."

Tess's heart skipped. She knew she did not dare turn her gaze away, and she forced herself to keep meeting his eyes. Any joy she felt at his change of heart began rapidly to drain away. "I didn't mean it to be that way," she said.

He took two steps toward her. He stood over her now, looking down. "Bunny's only seventeen, Miss Avery. She can't resist all the lures you're holding out. If I stand in her way, God knows what she might do."

Tess felt cornered. And the half-light in the apartment seemed suddenly ominous. She didn't like him looming over her that way. With one fluid motion she boosted herself out of the chair over its arm, and started toward the light switch. She intended to turn on the lights, bustle into the kitchen, do anything except be stared down by this tall and hostile man.

He was quicker than she. He moved in front of her, blocking her way. "Don't try to walk out on me. You're going to hear this."

"I'm just trying to put some light on the subject," she objected. "And make some coffee. We can sit at the table and discuss this like civilized—"

She had tried to move past him, but his hands were on her upper arms, holding her in place. His nearness suddenly seemed smothering to Tess, filling her with dizzy urges and tingling apprehension.

"I don't want coffee," he said, bending nearer so that she had to look into his eyes again. "And you can't shed any light on the subject. It's too murky. And I don't feel civilized about this, so I won't talk that way."

She knew better than to fight him. She willed her body to be still, and her only motion was to raise her head higher so that her look was almost haughty. "You're in the city now," she said quietly. She glanced pointedly at his hands on her arms. "Shouldn't you forego the wilderness tactics?"

His grip tightened hard enough to make her inhale sharply. "I'm trying to tell you that my niece is in a vulnerable position. I'm not signing your stinking releases to indulge her. I'm signing them so she won't run off and make the mistake of her life. Like her mother did."

Tess looked at him in surprise. What did he mean? What mistake had Bunny's mother made?

"Her mother?" she asked. All she knew was that Bunny's mother, Cal's sister, was dead.

He ignored the question. He said nothing. He only shook his head, as if the subject was best not spoken of.

His silence filled her with greater frustration than before. "Your niece is a talented girl, whether you like it or not," Tess said. A spark of anger had fanned to life in her, and she could feel it growing. "There's no temptation to it. You can stand in her way or you can decide not to stand in her way. You know it, she knows it, I know it."

"She's also a willful young woman. And a devious one. All I'm trying to do is keep her under control a while longer. Until, God willing, she grows up a little more. Right now she's full of crazy big ideas and has this boyfriend worse than she is—only he's no boy, and that makes things worse."

"Is wanting to leave home and pursue a career such a crazy big idea?" Tess challenged. "Lots of women do it these days. The dark ages are over—haven't you heard?"

He brought his face closer to hers and spoke from between clenched teeth. "I've heard. And the world's full of drugs and crazy people and ruthlessness and enough evil to gobble up a thousand inexperienced girls like Bunny. Bunny's cunning—but she doesn't have a lot of sense. She's just smart enough to think she's a lot smarter than she is. And hooked up with this idiot that's flattering and chasing her—"

"Her boyfriend?" Tess asked. She gave a bitter little laugh. "I think you're jealous. Is that it? Some dark, Freudian thing? You've raised this girl, and you can't stand to see some other man take her away? You can't bear to lose control of her life?"

He straightened to his full height. The hands on her arms went as still as metal bands. "Ah. A sick insinuation. I might have expected it."

Tess glared up at him. "What's so wrong with this man? Bunny's an individual—she ought to be able to love whatever person she wants."

Even in the shadowy light she could see his expression harden into even greater disgust. His mouth curled up at one corner and when he spoke, the passion in his voice was bitter. "Fred Fortescue is almost thirty years old. He's a professor at the college, for God's sake. What kind of professor takes up with a girl almost half his age and still in high school? I'll tell you what kind—one as silly as she is.''

Tess flinched slightly. Even at her most charitable, she had to admit that Fortescue didn't sound like the sort of man she would want pursuing a seventeen-year-old girl, especially one as unpredictable as Bunny.

Cal saw the doubt clouding her face and went on relentlessly. ''The fool studied television in college, so he thinks he'll be a star if he can just make it out of Nebraska. He's vain, he's weak, and there are probably poodle dogs running around out there that have a firmer grasp on reality than Fred. But there he is, skulking around, telling Bunny what a genius she is, and what a genius he is, and what a reactionary, tyrannical old crank I am.''

Tess tried to shrug philosophically. ''Well, you shouldn't get excited. She'll probably outgrow it. The worse fuss you make about him, the more wonderful she'll be convinced he is.''

He shook his head in impatience. A dark lock of hair fell over his forehead, making him look even more angry than before. ''Don't you think I know that?'' he demanded. ''But ever since he got wind of this calendar thing, he's been telling Bunny how wonderful and talented she is and blowing it all out of proportion. Now, thanks to you, he's found out about the magazine thing, and he's played on her ego like a violin. Nothing would give me more pleasure than to tell you no about that damned magazine, Miss Avery. But if I do, I'll drive Bunny right into that fool's arms.''

Tess signed. Fatigue and confusion filled her. Worse, Cal's nearness, the warmth of his tall body, the raw intensity of him, unsettled her until she could no longer think straight. ''Just let go of me, will you,'' she said, her voice shaking. ''I'm not your niece. You don't have to hang on to me.''

He did not let go, but he used one hand to raise her chin so that she had to look into his face again. The eyes that had seemed so impassioned before now had a different expression. She could not tell what it was—weariness, perhaps, or even tenderness.

"I don't want her to ruin her life," he said, his voice low. "That's all you need to understand. I don't want her to end up like—like somebody else I knew."

His hand rested lightly along her jaw, and for the first time Tess understood the depth of his emotion. He loved his niece, and he was fighting hard to keep her from doing something foolish and self-destructive. Something had happened to his sister, and it haunted him.

"I'll sign your releases," he said. His eyes had grown hard again, but the fingers touching her face were still gentle. "Just leave her alone. All right? Don't meddle anymore. The situation's too critical."

"I—" Tess began, then tried to turn her face away. He would not let her.

"Not leave *me* alone," he emphasized. "Leave *her* alone. She's too young. She's too vulnerable. She isn't ready for this kind of thing. Promise me."

"I—" she began again, searching for words. The fierce eyes, the gentle hand made conflicting emotions swarm through her. "The thing's gotten out of hand. I'm sorry. I'll do my best—"

He moved a fraction of an inch closer to her, bending nearer. "No. Your promise. Leave her alone."

She tried to move his hand away, but instead he captured hers, his fingers lacing through her own. His face was so near hers that she could feel its warmth. "Promise," he said.

"I'll do the best I can," she said, turning from him in confusion. He released her partially but kept hold of her hand. She stepped as far away as she could, but he still held her fingers locked in his, and he stared down at her, waiting for her to say more.

"That's all I can say," she said, looking away from him again. "I have a job to do. I never meant to do anything more than that, whether you believe it or not. But you should know that you can't protect her forever. She's an extraordinary girl. And the world's going to keep calling her to come away. You have to accept that."

She tried to draw farther away, but still he held her. Their arms were extended like two people who have struggled to reach each other or are struggling to break away. "Is that what happened to you?" His voice was low. "The world called you away from that farm in Frontier County?"

She still didn't look at him. She stared at her bare feet instead. *Twenty-six years old,* she thought, *and still going barefoot.* Maybe she hadn't come so far away from the farm after all.

"The great world called," she said with weary sarcasm. "Maybe you don't know how sweet that call can sound. Certain people—my father—tried to keep me back. It doesn't work. Believe me."

She said no more. She had no wish to discuss her father with Cal Buchanon or anyone else.

He kept her hand in his, and she felt as if his touch transmitted a dangerous tickle of electricity down her arm and into the core of her spine.

His voice was just as quiet as before. "Did it ever occur to you that maybe he loved you?"

She gave him a sidelong glance. The memory of her quarrels with her father made her want to shut off all her emotions, walk away from them. "No," she said shortly. "It didn't."

"Typical," he said, looking across the shadows at her. "So you left. For—this." He made a satiric gesture with his free hand to indicate the barren apartment.

"Not this," she countered. "I'll be leaving this, too. I'll be going to New York one of these days."

He moved closer to her until he stood directly in front of her again. Still he did not release her hand. Tilting her chin, he raised her face to his again. "Why aren't you there already?"

"What?" she asked, confused by both his question and his touch.

"If you wanted to go so badly, why aren't you already there? Why have you stayed here?" His gaze fell to her mouth, lingering there. The lamplight made his lashes cast shadows on his cheekbones.

Her senses were in a tumble of conflict. "It just hasn't been the right time. I have debts to pay off. I have no connections in New York, nothing guaranteed when I get there. People don't just plunge into something like that."

"Don't they?" he taunted. His thumb moved along the curve of her cheek, tracing its softness. "I thought that's exactly what they did."

"Look," she said in frustration, "would you stop touching me? Just stop, will you?"

But she made no move to escape him. His fingers were in her hair now, gathering the silkiness and caressing it. "Plunging in is what Bunny wants to do. It's what Fred Fortescue should have done years ago, only he's too cowardly. Are you a coward, too? Is that why you never got any closer to New York than Omaha?"

"I—" Tess muttered, finding it hard to breathe again, "I—"

"Maybe you don't want to leave this place as far behind as you think," he drawled, toying with a curl that tickled her ear. His upper lip twisted, partly in scorn, partly in amusement. "Maybe you're not quite as sophisticated as you think."

He seemed to be moving even nearer to her, and Tess's heart felt as if it were going mad within her chest, beating so hard that it cut off her breath. His hand was on the back of her neck now, his fingers still lacing through the soft cloud of her hair.

"I—" said Tess. His face drew nearer still to hers. "I—"

"You, my dear," he breathed, taking her face between his hands, "look beautiful in your fancy clothes. But you were born to wear blue jeans. They fit you like your skin."

Distance between them vanished. He kissed her.

CHAPTER EIGHT

TESS WAS too alarmed either to resist or respond to his kiss. The warmth of his lips against her own dizzied her with desire, yet frightened her as well. The feelings he awoke were too intense to be safe. They threatened to shake her carefully planned world to trembling bits.

His hands were on her shoulders, drawing her more intimately against his long body. Almost against her will, Tess rose onto her tiptoes to taste more deeply of his kiss. Once again she had the irrational conviction that his mouth fit against hers as perfectly as if it had been designed to do so.

Once he had kissed her angrily, with hunger but no tenderness. Once he had kissed her seductively, intending to bewitch her. But this time it was different. He kissed her as if he couldn't help himself, and there was something bittersweet in it.

Tess understood, because she didn't want to kiss him either, but she felt powerless to break away from him. It seemed inevitable that they touch so, that he hold her so.

She started to raise her hands to lay them against the crisp front of his shirt but stopped herself. The taste of him, the feel of him was driving her slightly mad. She did not dare bring herself into any closer contact.

He seemed to sense her reluctance and drew back slightly, staring down at her. His hands gripped her shoulders more tightly. "I don't understand you," he breathed. "I think you're frightened. Of what? I'm the one who should be running for my life."

Troubled, he studied the defenseless softness of her mouth, the worry that shadowed her eyes. She suddenly seemed young to him, far younger than she really was. He could tell that she wanted him to kiss her again. He could also tell that she was scared to death he'd do exactly that.

He'd specialized in women who knew the difference between love and sex. He'd thought she was one of them, but now he had the unsettling certainty she was not. Too many feelings shone out of her face, and they disturbed him more than he wanted.

She shook her head wordlessly and said nothing. He moved his hands up to frame her face, smoothing her hair back. "I don't want this to happen," she managed to say, her voice broken.

He hadn't wanted it to happen, either. Still, once more, he brushed her hair back. "Why?" he asked, his voice harsh. "You have other plans?"

She nodded but trusted herself to say no more.

He let his hands fall to her shoulders again. The line of his mouth grew perturbed. He had thought he'd known exactly what she was. Now he was no longer sure. "Who are you?" he questioned, frowning. "The barefoot farm girl in jeans who's afraid of a kiss? Or the career woman determined to go up in the world—no matter what it takes? Which one? I swear I can't tell."

Tess gazed at his handsome shadowy face as if hypnotized. She wanted to escape from him, pretend he had never existed. Paradoxically she wanted to stay there, lost in his eyes forever. "I'm both of them," she said at last.

A nerve twitched in his cheek. His face grew grimmer than before. "And which one is afraid of me?"

"Both," she said and looked away. Her emotions were so complex she no longer understood them herself.

"Why?" His hands were moving restlessly on her shoulders.

She swallowed. "You remind me of too much. You're what I had to leave behind."

He was silent a moment. Then he nodded, as if he understood. "You see me the way Bunny does, don't you? As some sort of bull-headed dictator—dangerous, unfair, oppressive. That's why you always defend her."

She shrugged noncommittally. She knew he was at least partly right. Cal frightened her because he was like her father. He was strong and stubborn, and he had the power both to stand in her way professionally and to hurt her personally.

He spoke from between clenched teeth. "But Bunny's a child. You're a woman. Can't you see I only want to protect her?"

She shrugged again, still not looking at him. "Sometimes people protect other people to death. Sometimes they try to live other people's lives for them."

He gripped her more tightly. He brought his face closer to hers, even though she still refused to look at him. She could feel the warmth of his nearness. It seemed to burn against her cheek. "And sometimes people don't know what's good for them," he said.

"Exactly what my father used to say," Tess retorted, her eyes flashing as she met his again. "He said I had big ideas and didn't know what was good for me. He said I had 'delusions of grandeur' and that a woman should 'keep her place.' He said I really didn't *need* an education. It was *wasted* on women—"

"Tess," Cal said sternly, "that's not what I'm like, and you know it. Sometimes I think you've never really seen me. And maybe I've never seen you until tonight. Once I thought about asking to start this over from the beginning. Maybe—maybe—" his voice trailed off in exasperation. He shook his head.

She ignored his statement because it was more comfortable to ignore it. Part of her wanted to be in his arms again. Part of her wanted to flee him as she had fled her father. She had fought hard for her freedom, so hard that she was almost exhausted.

"Well," she said, her throat tight, "I'm living my own life, my own way. And sooner or later, Bunny will, too. Whether you like it or not."

"You call this living life your own way?" he demanded and made an angry gesture that took in the bare little apartment.

"Yes," she countered, offended. "I have college loans to pay off. Medical bills, too. I had appendicitis my last year of school—and hardly any insurance. I have to live within my means. Besides, I have plans. Places to go, things to do. So what?"

"Nothing," he said. He released her shoulders and turned away, disgust in the motion. "Nothing. Live however you want. Live in New York. Or live in a tree. It's not my concern. Look, I've got to go. I'm sorry things got out of hand—as usual."

"As usual, Mr. Buchanon, we've brought out the worst in each other," she returned as coolly as she could. "But at least the magazine issue's resolved."

He tossed her a glance that told her he was not happy about the way it had been resolved. Irritably he pushed his hand through his hair, brushing his unruly forelock into place. His mouth took on an impatient crook.

"I meant what I said about your staying away from Bunny. And I suppose I owe you an apology. When I first met you, I thought you were using sex as a ploy. But I don't think you even understand sex. You're afraid of emotion. Under that icy facade there may still be a woman with feelings, but you're so bitter about the past, she's dying fast.

That's right, dying. Too bad. If you'd let her live, she might have been—something."

He gave her a look that was partly scathing, partly bemused, and left. His quick footsteps descended the stairs. She heard his car start and the sound of him backing out of the drive.

For some reason she didn't understand, she kept staring at the door through which he'd left. Hesitantly she lifted her fingers and touched her lips, which still tingled from his kiss.

Then, to her amazement, she burst into tears without knowing why.

Why was she crying? she asked herself in perplexity. Why did she care what he said about her or what he thought of her? He had set her free. She was going to New York.

"I DON'T KNOW what's wrong with you," Delia complained during their coffee break. "You've got the world by the tail. You brought off that deal between Heritage Foundation and the magazine, and you didn't have to do a thing. Mrs. Madigan thinks you're the greatest thing since sliced bread. As soon as that New York job opens, you know she'll recommend you. You're practically on your way. What's your problem?"

"I don't have a problem," Tess said. "I just haven't been sleeping well, that's all."

"Mmm," Delia said, cocking an eyebrow. "Just like those Macbeth folks in the play. Are you guilty about something?"

"Of course not," Tess replied. In truth she felt guilty about a great deal—things she'd done, things she hadn't done, things she'd said, things she hadn't said.

She was willing to reap the rewards that would fall to her because Cal had changed his mind, although she knew he had changed it only because she had created such chaos in his life. She had let Cal kiss her, and almost as bad, she had told him far more about her feelings than she had meant to. His insights about her stung, and now she spent her nights thinking about what she should have said to him.

"Well," Delia said, nibbling on a Danish pastry, "I don't know what happened between you and that Buchanon man—"

"Nothing happened," Tess insisted. But she didn't look at Delia when she said it.

"But if I had a man that gorgeous appear on my doorstep on a Saturday night, I wouldn't sit around with gloom and doom written all over me."

"Oh, Delia," Tess said impatiently, "what difference does it make that he's good-looking? Sometimes I think people don't even really see the man. I mean they don't see that there's a person under all that—that 'gorgeousness.' No wonder he hates this calendar project."

"Hmm," Delia said and gave Tess a thoughtful look. "At first you said his looks were his only asset. At first you said he was a beast."

"He's not so bad." Tess shrugged. It made her sick to admit it, but she knew she had been unfair to him. He wasn't really like her father. He didn't want to crush Bunny's spirit or ambitions. He just wanted her to be less headstrong.

But, she thought glumly, he had been just as unfair to her. All the way through their muddled relationship they had misjudged each other, repeatedly and badly. It was as if they were cursed never to get along.

"I think I know what your problem is," Delia said, nodding and sweeping the crumbs from her Danish into a napkin. "Your problem is—"

"Your problem," said Mrs. Madigan, appearing in the doorway, "is that opportunity is practically kicking the door down, and both of you are oblivious to the noise."

"I believe my obliviousness has just come to an end," Delia said and rose to put her coffee cup away.

Tess gave a slight start. Mrs. Madigan's eyes were trained directly on her, and they glittered with excitement. *This has to do with me,* Tess thought with rising alarm. *And it probably has to do with Cal. Oh, no. Oh, please, no. Not again. Not any more.*

Mrs. Madigan entered the reception area and sat on the edge of Delia's desk. "This has to do with you, Tess," she said, adjusting one of the cuff links of her silk blouse. "And it has to do with Buchanon. I want you to take him to New York. And while you're there, you can interview for the job at the Chadwick Agency. It's just opened up."

Tess's lips parted in surprise. Mrs. Madigan had uttered no more than five sentences, but they seemed to contain more information than Tess's brain could process. "What?" she said.

Mrs. Madigan sighed, adjusted her other cuff link, then started over. "Aggy Chadwick phoned. That position I've told you about—it's opened up. I've recommended you for it. She wants you to come to New York and interview."

Behind Mrs. Madigan, Delia's eyes brightened with delight. She raised her hands above her head in the gesture of a champion.

Tess could only stare. Now that it had finally happened, she felt numb, almost empty. She managed to smile. "That's wonderful," she said.

"Yes," Mrs. Madigan agreed. "It is. And I'm the one who arranged it. In return, I want a favor. I want you to get the Buchanon man to New York. To appear on the Morty Jessen show. It's very important to the calendar project. And to Aggy Chadwick, I might add. Her nephew has just started a graphics company. He thinks a poster of the Buchanon man could have huge potential as a money-maker for us—and for him. It would be sort of a cooperative effort between his company and the Homestead Heritage Foundation. Aggy's *very* eager for her nephew to succeed."

"Wait a minute," Tess said, her mouth suddenly dry. She looked in panic at Delia, who no longer smiled, only sat at her desk, wariness in her eyes.

"Wait a minute," Tess repeated. "The Morty Jessen Show wants Cal Buchanon as a guest? That's the highest rated talk show on television...."

"Correct," Mrs. Madigan agreed with a cool smile. "Jessen has millions of viewers. And his people want Buchanon. All Buchanon has to do is go on, look wonderful, show a few pictures and plug the calendar. It'll increase sales by tens of thousands."

Tess's mind spun. "How—how did they even find out about him? About the calendar?"

Mrs. Madigan smoothed her silver hair. "One of the editors at *Modern Woman* knows one of the staffers at Jessen's show, happened to show her the picture—well, Jessen does theme shows. He's doing one on hunks. Who better than Buchanon?"

Who indeed? thought Tess dismally. Cal seemed likely to throttle anybody who called him a "hunk" to his face. She licked her dry lips. "Mrs. Madigan, he'll *hate* this idea. He's going to say no. He agreed to sign the releases only if I left him and his family alone. Completely alone."

Mrs. Madigan's smile faded. "It's for a good cause. It's for what I believe in. I would hate at this late date for Aggy Chadwick to see you really can't deliver the goods."

Tess rose from the flowered armchair, her hands extended in a gesture of helplessness. "The man isn't *goods,* Mrs. Madigan. He's a human being. A very stubborn one that we've probably pushed too far already."

"Bother his stubbornness," Mrs. Madigan almost spat. "He's already signed the releases. They came in the mail this morning. He can't back out on us, or I'll have him in court so fast his head will spin.''

Once more Tess's eyes met Delia's in a tense exchange. Then she returned her gaze to Mrs. Madigan. When the woman chose, she could have a stare as unwavering as a cobra's.

"Mrs. Madigan, I don't think you understand,'' Tess said as evenly as possible. ''Cal Buchanon won't do a television show. We can't force him to do it. And he's not going to like the poster idea, either. I can almost guarantee you he won't cooperate.''

"Tess,'' Mrs. Madigan said, her eyes colder than before, "I don't think *you* understand. Your job is to *make* him cooperate. I want him on that show, plugging that calendar. And Aggy Chadwick wants him on that poster for her nephew's sake. I do, too, for the foundation's sake. You, as I remember, want to go to New York. You do *not* want to displease either Aggy Chadwick or myself. Do you, dear?''

Tess took a deep breath. "No, ma'am,'' she said, "I don't. But—''

"Good,'' Mrs. Madigan said in the cooing tone that Tess was learning to hate. "I've taken the liberty of calling up there already. To the Buchanon residence. I've explained things to the niece.''

Tess's eyes widened in horror. If she'd felt numb and hollow before, now she felt as if someone had knocked all the wind out of her, and it hurt.

"Oh, no,'' she breathed. "You shouldn't have talked to her. Not the niece. Oh, no. He'll hate us for this.''

"Who cares if he hates us?'' Mrs. Madigan asked brightly. "As long as he does what we want? One doesn't, as they say, make on omelet without breaking a few eggs. I suggest you go there and talk to him face to face. I imagine he's about to go into one of those boorish phases when he doesn't answer his phone.''

"But Mrs. Madigan—" Tess protested, her throat almost choked with resentment.

"Just remember," Claire Madigan said with her cool smile and cobra stare, "it's for such a wonderful cause. And your own good, too, of course. This man is standing in your way—and mine. He must, of course, be dealt with."

She turned and left the room, her back ramrod straight.

"Of course," Tess said numbly. She turned to Delia. "Oh, Delia—what do I do now?"

Delia examined Tess's stricken face. "If I were in your position," she said with perfect seriousness, "I believe I would brush up on my praying."

TESS'S CAR, in spite of its recent repairs, still commanded a frightening vocabulary of rattles, gasps, wheezes, clunks and moans. Delia, knowing Tess feared being stranded in Lawler again, insisted Tess take her car, a new silver Taurus sedan.

"Don't let the Buchanon man shoot any holes in it," Delia warned. Tess thought she was only half joking.

The day was one of those jewellike Nebraska days that was almost too perfect. But none of its beauty comforted Tess. Her conscience, uneasy before, twisted as painfully now as if on a torturer's rack.

Mrs. Madigan had put her into an impossible position. By telling Bunny before Cal, the woman had made sure the new issues would stir up as much conflict as possible in the family. Tess had been foolish enough to tell Mrs. Madigan that Cal had agreed to the magazine releases to keep Bunny in line, that he didn't want her rebelling by running off with Fred Fortescue.

What Mrs. Madigan had done was no better than blackmail, and Tess had made it possible. Cal would have every right to be angry and resentful—and uncooperative. She sensed he had been pushed to the limit trying to accommodate Bunny. He would hate both Tess and the Madigan agency for trying to push him further.

She had a choice, she told herself. She could turn Delia's car around and go back to Omaha. She had sent out job applications. She didn't have to be involved in this nasty muddle any longer. Something else would turn up.

But the something else, whatever it might be, wouldn't take her to New York, at least not for a long time. Her father had told her once in anger that she would never get as far as New York. Her brothers had teased her unmercifully about going to any city at all. And somehow, worst of all, Cal had told her that if she'd really wanted to go to New York, she'd be there by now.

Her hands tightened on the steering wheel. She wanted so badly to go, to show them all. She didn't want to live out her life and someday look back and say she'd never had the courage to take her shot at the big time.

But, she thought, the choking sensation strangling her throat again, did she want it this badly? Badly enough to exploit Bunny's weakness and manipulate Cal? Badly enough to sow seeds of strife in an already troubled family?

A coldly logical part of her mind told her that Mrs. Madigan was right—it was all for a good cause. The calendar project had sprung from the highest of motives. Didn't Cal have a moral duty to help as much as he could? Hadn't he brought this on himself by being so damnably uncooperative all the way? Shouldn't he admit that if Bunny was headed for disaster, he couldn't save her? Couldn't he just see that Bunny would have to make her own mistakes?

Tess shook her head, too confused to arrive at any answer except one. She didn't feel good about what she was doing. No matter how fine the cause, or how much depended on it, she didn't feel good at all. But after what Mrs.

Madigan had done, Tess owed it to Cal to meet him face to face. She had no idea what she would say to him.

CAL'S HOUSE seemed almost deserted when Tess pulled into the drive. Evening was falling, and the only light was the golden square of one kitchen window.

She saw no sign of Cal or Bunny or even the dog. Apprehensively she got out of Delia's car and walked up the porch steps. The cool breeze coming off the fields smelled so clean and fragrant it made the knot in Tess's throat swell more tightly. She could smell the alfalfa in bloom.

Standing before the front door, she raised her hand, paused, then knocked.

A long moment of silence answered her before she heard the sound of someone moving toward the door, and she took a deep breath in case it was Cal.

The door swung open, and Tess was relieved to see Edna. But Edna's solemn face clearly said that Tess was not welcome. The older woman looked as beautiful and dignified as ever in her crown of gray braids, but her expression was disapproving. "Miss Avery," she said with a sigh of exasperation. "He said you'd be back, Cal did. He said he'd told you not to come back—but that you would." She shook her head.

"Edna," Tess said anxiously, "I want you to know that I wasn't responsible for the call to Bunny. I knew nothing about it. I didn't want to come here again, but it's my job—"

"If you've done nothing wrong, then you needn't try to excuse yourself," Edna said shortly.

Tess had the decency to blush. "Where's Bunny?"

"In her room. Crying. So emotional her stomach's aching. I imagine you know why. Now she's got it in her head that she could see New York if only Cal would let her. That terrible woman, that Mrs.—Mrs.—"

"Madigan," Tess supplied.

"Madigan," Edna said with scorn. "She implied that Bunny's photograph would be used for that poster they want to make. Bunny's practically hysterical that Cal doesn't want to do it. She keeps saying, why can't he be like that Fred person and understand her? Poor Cal. I wish I'd never pushed him into this. He was right. I was wrong. He should never have gotten involved."

"Edna," Tess said, "I'm terribly, terribly sorry. But I've got to talk to him. Will you let me?"

Edna nodded without enthusiasm. "Of course. He wants to talk to you. He's in the barn. In the hayloft. It's that way." She gestured toward the back door.

"I know," Tess said and started in that direction. This time she was prepared. No matter where he went, field or corral, pasture or barn, she was prepared to follow. She had stopped at home and changed into her jeans, a green plaid blouse and the battered cowboy boots she had worn years ago.

She went out the back door and crossed the barnyard swiftly, her strides long, her head down. It was a determined pace, and it belied how nervous she felt. In the dark fragrance of the barn she paused a moment to let her eyes adjust. Then she headed for the ladder that led into the hayloft.

"Mr. Buchanon?" she called as she climbed. "Edna says you're up here? I'm sorry, but we need to talk."

There was no answer. Beneath her in the shadows a horse nickered softly. She climbed into the loft and stood, brushing hay from the knees of her jeans. The big loft door was open, looking out on the western field where the quarter horses and the Tennessee walkers grazed. The sun had nearly set, filling the sky with gold rapidly fading to gray.

She saw Cal, standing, leaning his elbow against a hay bale. He stared moodily at the darkening sky. He wore jeans, a blue work shirt and well-worn boots of tooled leather.

"Cal?" she said softly and cursed herself when her voice broke. Her throat was choked more badly than before.

"Come here and sit," he ordered. He didn't look at her. He kept staring out the open door. Somewhere in the barn rafters a pigeon cooed and fluttered. Beneath them the horse nickered again, then blew softly.

She waded through the ankle-deep hay and sat on a bale near him. It had been years since she'd been in a hay loft. She'd forgotten how much she'd loved them, their coziness, their quiet and their sense of secrecy.

He glanced at her, taking in the plaid shirt with its rolled up sleeves, the faded jeans, the brown boots. "Well," he muttered. "You fooled me again. I thought you'd probably be climbing into the loft wearing an evening gown or something."

She had her hands clasped together in her lap. She leaned toward him earnestly. "I knew nothing about that call Mrs. Madigan made to Bunny. I didn't want to come here. But the call's been made, and this is my job. I don't exactly like it very much right now. And I want to tell you that I'm sorry for causing you more trouble. I—I know how you feel about your niece."

"It doesn't seem to make any difference," he said, his tone acid. "You also knew I wanted her left alone."

Tess nodded guiltily. "But I wasn't the one—"

His lip curled in a snarl. "You must have told somebody that Bunny could be played and used to get to me—I'm sick of this, Avery. Bloody, stinking sick of it."

Tess hung her head. She stretched out her foot and examined her scuffed boot. "I'm sick of it myself."

"But not so sick you'll stop all this—this damned manipulation. Oh, no. Not that sick. Because this is how you get to New York. God, you must want it badly. I wished I wanted something that much. But I never did. Except to mind my own business and get those kids raised. I almost made it. Then you came along.''

She shrugged, a futile gesture. ''I've actually thought about not going—''

''Is that supposed to impress me?'' he practically hissed at her. ''Oh, you'll go. If you don't get it out of your system, it'll haunt you till you go crazy from it. I've seen it before. I just didn't know I'd be condemned to see it again and again. It's like watching reruns from hell.'' He swore and turned from her.

She picked up a straw and began to twist it aimlessly. ''Listen,'' she said, not looking at him, ''I know you don't want to do the show. Or the poster. I know you probably won't. And that means I won't get to New York. Not yet, at least. But that's all right. I'll get there eventually. In the meantime, I guess all I can do is tell you how sorry I am. And if you don't want to get involved in this latest madness—well, maybe I can help you explain to Bunny. She might listen better to somebody from outside the family.''

He shot her a short, scathing look. ''So that's why you're here in your equivalent of ashes and sackcloth? To humble yourself? That's interesting. I wouldn't have expected that, either. Unfortunately, it's not necessary. This time I won't fight.''

He stared out at the horizon again. A single star shone high in the dusky sky.

He had that dangerous air about him again, she thought, that aura of a powerful animal in a weak cage, of a man filled with barely contained intensity. ''What do you mean?'' she asked. She rose and went to stand beside him.

He had his thumbs hooked into his back pockets. He took a deep breath of the evening air. ''I mean I'm going to New York. I'll do their stupid show. Maybe I'll even do their stupid poster. I don't know. If it helps Bunny. . . .''

She looked at him, frankly astonished. "You will? But why? I thought you'd never—"

He wheeled to face her, staring down angrily, his thumbs still in the back pockets. "What I never thought was that I'd be surrounded by so many devious, scheming, blood-sucking women. I've got a kid in that house—" he pointed angrily in the direction of his house "—that I have every reason to believe is planning to elope with that idiot Fred Fortescue. She thinks that I don't understand her, but that he does. He wants to take her to New York—where they'll become great artists together. Ha! Well, if she's determined to see New York, it better not be with him. She'll either end up supporting him, or they'll both starve. I'll do whatever it takes to defuse this firecracker. Believe me. Whatever it takes."

"But—" Tess said, confused. "I thought you were determined not to give in to her or spoil her."

"This is war, dammit," he said. "And in war a man does what he has to. She's determined to have a career—all right. I'll do what I can for her. But she's not going to ruin her life by marrying that moron, that clown, that jackass—not if I can help it."

Tess shook her head in disbelief. "You mean you'll go through with it? You'll go to New York? You'll do the show? And maybe the poster?"

He nodded, his face stormy. "Yes. But on my terms. First, on that show, I don't answer any stupid 'hunk' questions. I talk about what kind of help the farmers and ranchers in this state really need. And if I'm on the poster—" he made a grimace of distaste— "it's one of Bunny's pictures. If she's really going into this thing, she'll need some photo credits. And when I bring her back here, I want to find a good photographer to apprentice her to. If she won't go to college, at least she can get some on-the-job training.''

Tess looked up at him, and saw how irate his handsome face was. "I—I could help," she said. "Find a photographer, I mean. I know most of the good ones—and I'd be glad to help—''

He looked at her, his lip curling again. "You've helped enough, Avery." With a sudden motion he seized her right hand and brought it to his lips. "You've helped more than enough. And I salute you."

He kissed her on the back of the wrist, then on the inside. His lips were warm and made her pulse jump.

"You've made more trouble for me that any woman I've met in the last fifteen years. And the maddening thing is that you stand there looking so innocent that I almost believe you could be. Except, of course, if you were innocent, you wouldn't be here at all. I hear—if Bunny's garbled version is true—that you're supposed to be with me in New York?''

"Yes." She nodded unhappily. She wished he'd let go of her hand. Her wrist burned where he had kissed her, and he looked not only handsome, but darkly menacing in the fading light.

He raised her inner wrist to his mouth again. He gave it a lingering kiss, but his eyes were on her face. "Why?" he asked, lowering her hand but not releasing it. "Are you my guardian? To keep the savage Nebraskan in hand in the big city? To make sure I behave?''

"I don't know." The light in his dark eyes gave her a genuine chill. "Maybe I am."

He smiled. It was a smile with no mirth, but Tess imagined she saw danger in it. He had captured both her wrists now and raised them once more to his lips. "Then your work's cut out for you. Because I don't plan to behave. Not at all.'' He kissed both her hands, then dropped them, a contemptuous gesture.

He walked away and descended the ladder. She was left standing alone, the prairie twilight behind her turning to blackness.

CHAPTER NINE

NEW YORK made Tess dizzy, Bunny giddy, and Cal grim. Edna, who loved quiet, refused to come at all. She had stayed at home, happy to listen to the meadowlarks, scent the new-mown alfalfa and watch as the sunlight dappled the fields in different ways at different times of the day.

"The only smart one in the whole bunch," Cal muttered about Edna's decision to stay behind. He said it over lunch in a trendy little restaurant in the Village. The restaurant was narrow, crowded, dark and viciously expensive. The food, however, was excellent; the etchings on the dark walls authentic, and the waiter haughty enough to convince Tess that she had no right even to be in the same city as he.

"This potato soup's cold," Bunny complained.

"It's vichyssoise," Cal muttered. "It's supposed to be cold." He wore a gray summer suit, and Tess supposed that he was the handsomest man in New York. Even the jaded residents of Manhattan had turned and stared at him on the streets. He had gritted his teeth and steadily ignored them.

Now his attention was trained on Bunny, who was toying with her soup spoon. "Look," Cal said to her, "you wanted to have the whole New York experience. Food is part of it. Would you have been happier if I'd taken you for a hamburger?"

"Probably," Bunny answered, taking a reluctant sip of her vichyssoise.

"It doesn't hurt to expand your tastes," Tess admonished as gently as she could. She'd felt like a bit of a bumpkin herself when she'd looked at the menu and had been surprised at how confident Cal seemed with the surroundings.

Bunny pushed her soup away and contented herself with nibbling a piece of buttered bread. "It's just that I'm not materialistic," she said rather grandly. "Fancy food doesn't matter to me. My art is more important. Fred's the same way."

"Fred," Cal said darkly, but Bunny ignored him and looked dreamy.

When they left the restaurant, Bunny practically skipped down the sidewalk, dropping back sometimes to stare into windows, rushing ahead to catch sight of some new wonder, her camera always ready.

Cal leaned over to mutter in Tess's ear, "You can take the girl off the farm, but you can't take the farm out of the girl. Even I didn't realize how naive she is. This kid isn't ready for this."

Tess, watching the joy on Bunny's face, wasn't so sure. The traffic, the noise, the crowded, towering buildings, the incessant crush of people, made her uneasy and Cal cheerless.

But vichyssoise aside, Bunny found delight in everything. The meanest street held enchantment for her.

They found the tiny studio of Mrs. Chadwick's nephew on a side street, sandwiched between an art gallery and a poster shop. The sign announced Pinxit Graphic Arts, William Chadwick Runes, President.

Will Runes was a wiry young man with tight blue jeans, a loosely flowing silk shirt and one dangling diamond earring. A long fringe of brown hair framed his balding head, and glasses perched on his narrow nose.

By the time Cal, Tess and Bunny crowded into his cluttered little office with him, there would hardly have been room to squeeze in a fly. Tess knew how sardines must feel, packed into their can.

She stared at the graphics taped and tacked to the walls, and Bunny stared at Will Runes as if he were as exotic as a man from Mars. Will, looking over the rims of his glasses, watched Cal with the objectivity of an artist examining an interesting subject. Cal, in turn, glowered with the frank dislike of a man who hates being stared at.

Will put his feet, which were clad in tattered running shoes, on his untidy desk. "You," he said, pointing at Cal, "have a face a camera loves. Have you got an agent? You could make a lot of money as a model. Or an actor. Can you act?"

Cal's mouth twisted with disgust. "I'd rather eat ground glass than act. Or, God forbid, model." He put such contempt in the word *model* that Will Runes winced slightly.

"Well," Will murmured, "you know I'm interested in doing a poster of you. The profits would be split equally between the Homestead Heritage Foundation and my company." He turned to Tess. "Those terms are agreeable to the foundation. Correct, Miss Avery?"

Tess nodded, and Bunny beamed, but Cal scowled and spoke before Tess could answer. "I don't think they're very good terms. You're asking the foundation for the favor. You ought to give them a better break. Otherwise, I'm not really interested."

Runes drew back in his chair slightly, clearly startled. Then he studied Cal again, calculation in his air. He obviously understood that he had an uncooperative subject on his hands. He also just as obviously believed that a picture of this man could bring his fledgling company a good deal of money.

He spoke slowly, thoughtfully. "I can see that this project is less than pleasant for you, Mr. Buchanon. I'd be willing, since the cause is a good one, to sweeten the offer.

Make a little sacrifice for charity." He turned to Tess again.
He smiled benignly. "How about giving the foundation a
somewhat bigger share, Miss Avery? Just to make sure this
is worth Mr. Buchanon's time. Make the split fifty-seven,
forty-three."

Tess opened her mouth to say that it would be wonderful, but once more Cal spoke before she had a chance to.
"Make it sixty-forty."

Tess and Bunny stared at him. Bunny looked as if she
wished to strangle him for interfering. Tess looked merely
horrified. The terms had already been set, and Will Runes
was being more generous than she could have hoped. Now
Cal sat, his arms crossed, looking stormy as a thunder-
cloud, making demands nobody had expected or approved.

Will eyed him warily. He took his feet from his desk. He
assumed a more dignified position and peered more nar-
rowly over the rims of his glasses. "Mr. Buchanon, I'm in
business for the same reason as anybody—to make a profit.
I believe in charity, but I believe it begins at home."

"So do I," Cal drawled. "And my home's Nebraska. I
want a sixty-forty split. For the folks at home. Take it or
leave it."

Tess felt Bunny stiffen beside her in a combination of
anger and embarrassment. Tess put her hand on the girl's
arm, signaling her to stay quiet. There was enough tension
in the little office without Bunny joining in the fray.

"Mr. Buchanon," Will said, removing his glasses, "you
don't seem to understand. I'm doing the foundation a very
great favor. This is an excellent opportunity for them."

Cal raised his eyebrows and gave Will a look that was
equally cool. "I understand. It's also an excellent opportunity for you. You're just starting out." He glanced around
the office and did not seem impressed. "You want a piece
of a project that's getting national coverage—press and

television. The publicity helps you. It costs you nothing. You don't lift a finger for it—the foundation supplies it. That's worth something. I say it's worth a sixty-forty split in the foundation's favor."

Will shook his head so that his long hair danced and his diamond earring twinkled. "No. Maybe they don't understand these things in Nebraska—"

"Maybe they don't understand these things in New York," Cal countered. "All you're doing is printing and distributing some posters. The picture's already taken. My niece took it."

Cal gestured toward Bunny who sat as stiffly as if cast from stone. "You're not paying her anything. You're not putting any money up front for the foundation. They've done everything so far. You've done nothing. It's my picture you want to use. You use it—you pay sixty per cent of the profits to the foundation. You also give my niece a photo credit on the poster."

"I can't do that," Will practically squeaked, his hair and his earring dancing with even more agitation. "I put my company name and the foundation's on the poster—that's it. This kid isn't even a professional. Why should I print her name on fifty thousand posters?"

What are you doing to us now? Tess wondered miserably, looking at Cal's steely face. *I've gotten you this far and now you're going to dig in your heels and be stubborn? You'll ruin everything for everybody.*

Cal's expression became even more obdurate. "You forget one thing, Runes. I don't want to be on your damned poster. You want me, make it worth my while. That means sixty percent for the foundation and photo credit for the girl. That's it."

Tess tensed, holding her breath. She could feel Bunny radiating irritable excitement beside her. Will took a deep breath and thrust his glasses back on with an abrupt movement. Tess could see the resentment burning on his face. She could also imagine the wheels spinning full-speed within his balding head. The rigid downward curve of his mouth made it clear that he did not like this tall man from the prairie dictating to him.

He opened his lips. Tess flinched, waiting to hear him say no.

"Fine," he said with a shrug. "What's the difference? I'll write it off my taxes anyway." He gave a more elaborate shrug. "I'll give the Homestead Heritage Foundation a break." He gave Bunny a hostile look. "You take a decent picture, kid."

Bunny, in one of her mercurial quick changes, had turned to sweetness and light again. "Yes," she said with a winning smile. "I do. Would you like to see more of them?"

"Not right now," Runes said sourly and cast an unpleasant glance in Cal's direction. He clearly did not want to deal any further with Cal, who drove too hard a bargain.

When Cal, Tess and Bunny were back outside again, Bunny looked up at her uncle with exasperation. "I thought you were going to ruin everything," she accused.

Tess still felt a bit weak, as if she had barely escaped a disaster. At the same time, a thrill of exhilaration tingled through her. Cal had taken a great risk, yet he'd won great stakes. He'd wrangled Bunny a credit and engineered ten per cent more of the poster's profits into the coffers of the foundation.

"I should have gone for seventy," Cal grumbled, frowning. "But he's a greedy SOB. I didn't want to push any harder."

"You shouldn't try things like that," Bunny scolded. "You don't know what you are doing."

"You got your photo credit, didn't you?" Cal asked, his voice cool.

Bunny was wrong, Tess thought, stealing a glance at the man beside her. Cal had known exactly what he was doing. And he had done it impressively. *Watch out, New York,* she thought. *This man means business.*

BUNNY CRINGED. Tess set her teeth and tried not to cringe.

"No," Cal said. "I won't do that."

The production assistant of the Morty Jessen show, a pretty blond women of about thirty, looked distraught.

"Listen," she said, a touch of panic in her voice, "it's what Morty wants. It's what his writers planned. The other men have agreed. We'll have a lot of fun."

"No," Cal repeated with an emphatic shake of the head. "I'm not taking my shirt off on national television. No way."

"But they've already written Morty's jokes," protested the assistant. She leaned across her desk imploringly. "We tape the show tonight. It's all set."

Cal sat back farther in his chair and crossed his arms in a gesture that Tess now recognized as a danger signal. "Tell them to change it."

"But everybody else is going along with it," the assistant pleaded. "We've got two models, a movie star and a Mister Universe contest winner. It's not as if you'd have to do it alone. See, Morty'll run it like a contest and be the MC—it'll be just for fun."

Cal shook his head. Bunny, sitting to his left, looked at him with frustrated resentment. Tess, seated at his other side, cleared her throat, then put her hand gingerly on the sleeve of his suit coat. "Cal," she began, hoping to caution him, then hated how thin and small her voice sounded.

He ignored her. "Maybe models and actors and Mister Universe don't mind taking off their clothes. I do. I'll talk about the calendar. I'll talk about the problems this country's farmers are facing. But I don't do beauty contests, dammit.''

The assistant looked as if she was going to cry. Her face turned red, her chin quivered, and her mouth began to twitch erratically. She glanced first at Tess, then at Bunny. "Morty's going to kill me," she said. "Can't somebody reason with this man?" She picked up a pencil and broke it in two, throwing the two halves on the desk in a gesture of pure frustration.

"I've been trying to reason with him for nearly eighteen years," Bunny said, her tone haughty. She gave her uncle a glance that was the chilling essence of adolescent disapproval.

"I think," Tess said carefully, "that Mr. Buchanon has a point." She had her hands in her lap and was twisting her fingers together nervously. "The other men make their livings by displaying their bodies. This is different."

"But we have a show planned on hunks—"

"Replan it," Cal said. "And don't call me a hunk. I came here to sell that silly calendar. And to say a thing or two about farming. You want to see my chest, show the picture from the calendar."

The assistant sagged slightly against her chair. She stared at him warily. "You don't mind if we show the photo? You're not going to be difficult if we do?"

Cal didn't look happy, but he nodded. "Show it. But only if you mention who took it. My niece, here." With a slight tilt of his head he indicated Bunny.

Bunny's frostiness melted. "I have lots of pictures." She smiled her most charming smile. "Lots and lots. You could show as many as you want. I could come on, too, and explain about them."

The assistant shot her a gloomy glance. "No thanks." The woman's eyes slitted as she returned her attention back to Cal. "Morty'd probably kick you off the show if he hadn't already used your picture as a teaser last night and in the ads all day today. Half the women in America are going to be tuning in to see you tonight. And Morty does *not* like to disappoint his audience."

Tess thought that Cal paled slightly when the blonde informed him that the picture had already been on television. But if the news disturbed him, he gave no other sign. He simply looked more determined than ever to do things his way.

Then his eyes flicked sideways a moment and met Tess's. They were cold and unforgiving. The message they shot to her was clear— *What sort of circus have you got me into this time, you crazy woman?*

EVEN BUNNY admitted that, although Cal's methods tortured the nerves, he seemed to know what he was doing. In the space of one day, he had procured two national credits for her. On the cab ride back to the hotel, she rewarded him with a smacking kiss to the cheek.

He put his arms around her, and as Tess watched the two of them she felt a pang deep within. She envied Bunny the ability to put that smile on Cal's lips, to fire that protective glint in his black-lashed eyes. Then she turned her gaze away, ashamed of her envy.

Cal despised everything Tess had got him into, she knew, but he was doing it, cooperating, for love. He was doing it to save Bunny. That he was the sort of man who could love so much made her feel empty, and it did odd, aching things to her heart.

She told herself not to think of love. There was business to be taken care of. The Morty Jessen Show still loomed before them, drawing closer every minute. Her stomach was in nervous, writhing knots.

So was Bunny's. She didn't want to go to the studio to see the show being taped. She pleaded fatigue and a stomach already exhausted by the day's emotional roller-coaster ride. She gave a hint, dramatically, that she had also perhaps been poisoned by cold potato soup.

"Too much excitement," Cal had muttered sardonically. "This town'd ruin anybody's stomach lining."

It was Tess who rode with him from the hotel in the limousine that the show provided. She wore a simple black silk dress and a single strand of pearls. Cal had given her a long look when he met her in the lobby, but he said nothing. He was ominously silent as the car purred through the crowded streets.

He hates every minute of this, Tess thought miserably. She didn't blame him. If he was nervous, it didn't show, and he didn't speak of it. He spoke of nothing whatsoever. He stared out the window of the limousine, his dark brows drawn together in a slight frown, lost in his own thoughts.

He wore a dark blue suit, a white shirt and a maroon-striped silk tie. One of Bunny's blond hairs gleamed on the shoulder of his jacket, and Tess could not keep herself from reaching over and picking it off. Even through the fabric she could feel the hardness and warmth of his shoulder.

He gave her the same brief look he had given her in the production assistant's office—unfriendly and unpardoning. His glance made the familiar emptiness stir within her, made her yearn for something that had no name. He returned his attention to the glut of traffic.

She could bear the stormy quiet no longer. "What are you going to say about the calendar?" she asked.

He shrugged, watching the congested street. "That I hope the money raised goes for reeducating people the farm crisis affects. People have got to stop depending on one cash crop. It's too risky. The first step is to learn to diversify. Stuff like that. I plan to be your basic crashing bore."

Tess sighed and stared at him. She didn't think he could be a bore no matter how hard he labored at it. He was too intense, too honest, too intelligent.

"You'll be fine," she said. She glanced up at him and resisted the urge to adjust his tie. "Are you worried about Bunny?"

She saw a muscle tick in his sun-bronzed cheek. "I'm always worried about Bunny. I've been worried about her since the day I took charge of her. The other two kids were a piece of cake compared to Bunny."

She swallowed hard. When she had first met Cal, she hadn't realized how difficult Bunny was. Keeping the girl on a straight and narrow path must be nightmarish. Tess knew now that she not only wouldn't relish the job, she couldn't do it. Bunny's will was too formidable. If she could be handled at all, it would only be by someone far stronger than herself. Someone like Cal.

"Are you worried about leaving her alone at the hotel?"

He nodded, still not looking at her. The line of his mouth was grim. "I can't watch her every minute. I have to trust her sometime. And if I can't trust her—well, that's that." He raised one shoulder in a stoic shrug.

Tess stared at her hands again. There was bitterness in Cal's voice, and something else besides, a note of profound regret that disturbed her to the center of her being.

He was right. Bunny was swiftly reaching an age at which no one could dictate to her. She would go her own heedless way, and the only person who could save her from folly would be herself. Cal could protect her from the world no more.

"Cal?"

He turned, his glance darkly questioning.

"What happened to Bunny's mother? To your sister? How did you end up with her children?"

He was silent for a moment. Then he nodded toward the streets. "Barbara? She came to conquer New York. She didn't."

"What do you mean?"

His elbow was on the armrest, his hand against his chin. The position gave him an air of thoughtfulness that was close to brooding. "She was a beauty. A true beauty. She thought she'd come here, make her fortune, be an actress. She didn't. She married an actor who never did any better than she did. Had three kids. Got a divorce. But didn't get any acting jobs. Started being an 'escort.' But things went from bad to worse for her. We didn't know. That, I guess, was the best acting job she ever did."

Tess stared at him in horrified disbelief. "Good Lord, Cal," she breathed. "She—she—" she couldn't bring herself to finish the sentence. It seemed to her that she had no right to finish it.

The muscle twitched in his jaw again. Slowly he turned so that his eyes met hers. "I mean she sold herself. She was a call girl. Her price kept going down. And finally she hit bottom. She'd already sent the kids home by then. Edna didn't know what was going on. Edna would never suspect such a thing. I was worried, but I didn't want to believe the worst. Too much else was going wrong."

He shook his head at the memories. "Our father was sick. He was dying, in fact. I was trying to keep the ranch going— hell, I *had* to keep it going. With the kids, there were six of us to support. Nights, I wrote my master's thesis. My father kept saying he wanted to live to see me get that degree. So I was breaking my back to do it all. No, I didn't want to believe anything bad could happen to Barbara. I couldn't let myself believe that. And then she died. Murdered."

His own face was impassive as he watched hers. He had said the word so calmly that at first it didn't really register on her consciousness. Then the shock of it struck her. Tess recoiled.

"Murdered?"

She could only stare at him. Oh, no, she thought. No wonder Cal had been so fiercely protective of Bunny, so determined to stand between her and danger.

"One of the hazards of her particular trade," he said between his teeth. "Well, it doesn't matter what she was. I loved her."

She tried to take a deep breath, but it caught painfully in her chest. "And the children? You kept the children?"

"I raised the kids," he said, biting off the words. He turned and stared out the window at the streets of New York again. "I owed her that. I couldn't save *her*, but I could take care of *them*."

The lines of his profile seemed almost severe in the dying light. His eyes seemed to be looking past the swarming streets, the crowd of buildings, searching for something lost deep in the past.

"And your father?"

"He died a month before Barbara did. In June. He lived to see me get the degree. And he died thinking she was an actress still waiting for her big break. He never knew, thank God."

"Oh, Cal," she said softly, laying her hand on his sleeve. "I'm sorry. It must have been hard for you to see this place—if it all happened to her here."

He didn't acknowledge her touch. "One of the last times I was here, I came to identify her. And bring her home. Home." He shook his head.

He set his jaw. "And the very last time I came here was for the trial. Of the man who killed her. It lasted a week. I'd sit in the courtroom all day, and at night I'd walk the streets, talking to her in my head. I was kind of crazy, I guess. I'd tell her about the kids. I'd tell her stupid things, like Bunny had lost another tooth and Marissa could never learn to spell *library*. I'd tell her everything was fine, we were taking care of everything. I hoped it was true."

He was quiet, then, with his same meditative air.

"The man who did it—he was convicted?"

He nodded. "Life in prison. No parole. It wasn't his first offense. And as soon as sentence was pronounced, I went back to the hotel and packed. I got out of there so that justice could be done and I wouldn't kill him myself. Because that's what I wanted to do."

He gave another bitter nod. "Yeah. That's what I wanted. But somebody did it for me. In prison. So he paid. At least he paid."

He fell back into his silence. The arm she touched was tensed and ominously still. She drew her hand away.

He turned and looked at her again. She felt naked under the force of his gaze. "You see?" he said, his mouth slanted bitterly. "There's another side to most things. Those people back in Nebraska you think were small-minded, who stood in your way, the ones you had to shake loose—maybe they didn't want to hurt you or crush you after all. Maybe they just loved you. Maybe that was their only sin. That they loved you."

This time it was her who turned her eyes away. She felt sick and hollow and didn't want him to see that she fought back tears. "I'm sorry," she said, her voice husky. "I'm terribly sorry about getting you involved in all of this—you *and* Bunny."

"It's a little late," he said, a touch of acid in his voice. "Come along, my little New Yorker. We're here. So let's try to make the bloody most of it."

The limousine had pulled up in front of the television studios. Signaling the chauffeur away, Cal took Tess's hand to help her from the car. She stood in front of the light-washed elegance of Rockerfeller Center, dressed in her finest, the handsomest man in New York at her side.

She had achieved her goal. She was in New York, and soon she would be staying, becoming a part of its power and grandeur.

She should have been aglow with happiness. Instead she had never been so miserable in her life. Unwittingly she had led Bunny to the edge of the very abyss that Cal had tried to keep her from for years.

ONE OF THE MAKEUP assistants sat on the greenroom sofa beside Tess, watching the television monitor. She had her fingers threaded through her hair and was pulling at it as if she were in pain. "Aaarrghhhh," she moaned, looking at Cal's image on the monitor. "I want to be joined to him for life. I want to have his children. Aaarrghhhh."

The blond production assistant sat glumly, slumped in a worn easy chair. "How can he be so charming on camera?" she demanded of no one in particular. "This afternoon in my office he was about as charming as a brick wall hit at ninety miles an hour. Now look at him. Every woman in America's going to be in love. I'm practically in love with him myself, and I don't even *like* him."

"Aaarrghhh," moaned the makeup girl again. "You can't be in love with him. *I'm* in love with him." She looked at Tess. "You're so lucky, I can't stand it. What's he *like*? He seems so smart. So sincere."

Tess stared at the monitor, more weighted with unhappiness than she had been before. Cal was handling himself well, resisting all of Morty Jessen's attempts to lure him into buffoonery or shallowness. The other men seemed vain, artificial and somehow trivial beside him.

She still had the sharp pain in her chest that kept her from breathing quite right. It made her voice sound strained. "He's smart. He's sincere. He's—it's hard to describe—he's responsible. When he says he'll do something, he does it. When he says he'll take care of something or someone, he'll do it. He cares about things. And people. And he's loyal. And strong. And moral."

"Why don't you just say he's perfect and be done with it?" the blond production assistant asked sarcastically. "Doesn't he have any faults at all?"

Tess sat, watching him on the TV screen. She remembered how contentious he had been when they met, how tumultuous their relationship had been. She felt her voice tighten still more. "Sometimes," she said softly, "he leaps to conclusions. But that's usually when he's tired. Or upset."

And I always managed to upset him, she thought. He must hate her to the marrow of her bones for dangling so many temptations in front of the impressionable Bunny.

"Aaagh," groaned the makeup girl, gripping handfuls of her hair again. "I mean it—this is love. It's real. It's everlasting."

No, Tess thought, the girl was babbling nonsense. She didn't love Cal. She saw only his surface. She herself, Tess realized with a pang, was the one who loved him. She loved him for what he was, not what he looked like. It had happened almost without her knowing it.

I love him, she thought, struck almost faint with wonder, yearning and regret. *What do I do now? I love him.*

She felt almost paralyzed by shyness as they rode back to the hotel in the limousine. For a long time Cal said nothing, only stared out at the multitude of lights that seemed to swirl around them. She did not trust herself to speak.

The back of the limousine had a corner niche designed to hold drinks, and in it someone from The Morty Jessen Show staff had placed glasses and a bottle of champagne in an ice bucket.

He gave out a rough sigh. "We may as well indulge," he said, and taking the bottle between his lean hands, he expertly popped the cork so that nothing exploded or fizzed out of control. He poured her a glass, then took one himself.

He raised his glass to her. "To it being almost over," he said.

She nodded and touched her glass to his. She tried to smile but couldn't. *Almost over,* she thought, the words haunting her. *Almost over.* It was excellent champagne, but it tasted bitter to her.

She could feel his eyes on her and was too conscious of his long body, sinewy and tough beneath the civilized cut of his clothes.

"This is, of course, the height of decadence," he said, watching her over the rim of his glass. "At least one of them. I suppose you like it."

He gave her a slight, slanted smile. She couldn't tell if it was friendly or sarcastic. "I don't know if I like it. I've never done it before—drunk champagne in a limousine, I mean."

"I imagine you'll get used to it." The smile grew a bit more friendly, or a bit more sarcastic; she couldn't tell which. "When's your job interview?"

"Tomorrow. At ten-thirty."

"Are you scared?"

"Terrified." The choking, painful sensation gripped her chest again.

He cocked a dark eyebrow. "That you won't get it?"

She shook her head. "I don't know. I really don't."

"Why were you so nervous tonight? Afraid I'd embarrass you and lose your job for you before you even got it?" A teasing note vibrated in his voice.

She shrugged and toyed with her false pearls. "I wasn't very nervous," she lied.

He laughed, and the sound sent prickles tingling along her nerves. "As soon as we walked into the studios, you turned green. And started swallowing all the time."

"I did not," she said, lying harder and hoping she sounded indignant.

"Better get used to it," he warned, the eyebrow cocking more wickedly. "It's going to be your world. What's the matter? You don't look as if it agrees with you."

"It agrees with me just fine," she said, lying with all her might this time. She cursed him for being the kind of man he was, for making her doubt what she'd wanted for so long.

"You can have it," he said, his smile vanishing. "Me, I'll be back on the ranch, mucking out stalls or checking fences or pulling some calf out of the creek. And I suppose I can have that, eh?"

"Actually," she said, her voice tight, "I'll miss it." She didn't like the vulnerable sound of that statement, so she added, "A little."

"A little." She was grateful that, as he spoke, he took his eyes from her and looked to the streets again.

"The Morty Jessen people," she said. "They want you to come back again. They told you that, didn't they? Would you? Ever come back to New York? Do it again?"

Her question hung in the air a moment, a long moment.

"No," he said, shaking his dark head. His voice was no longer mocking but was thoughtful. "No. Not unless there's something worth coming back for."

Her heart took another of its strange arhythmic beats. "And what would be worth coming back for?" she asked, her voice artificially flippant.

He turned so that once more, across the dim interior of the vehicle, his eyes met hers. As he studied her, the shadows told her that his mouth had taken on an odd slant. "I can't imagine," he said at last.

HE TOOK hold of her arm, out of politeness she supposed, as they entered the lobby of the hotel. The Morty Jessen Show staff had placed them in a fine hotel, and its lobby seemed to Tess to be all chandeliers, marble, deep carpet and fresh flowers.

"You were very good on TV," she told Cal, because she thought she should say something. Their ride had ended in uncomfortable silence. "You really were. You seemed completely at ease."

He gave her a wry quarter of a smile that made her heart dip, then race. "I was about as at ease as a man in a roomful of rattlesnakes."

He led her to the bank of elevators and punched one of the gleaming brass buttons. The ornate doors sighed open, and Tess and Cal entered the mirrored interior. She studied his reflection furtively as he loosened his tie and undid the top button of his shirt. "I want to get out of this suit and have a quick drink. I need it. And liquor that bubbles isn't liquor in my book."

"You were nervous? You didn't seem to be. Not a bit."

"You," he said, his voice stern, "can have a real drink with me. That champagne didn't seem to take you off edge a bit. Why *were* you so blasted nervous? Afraid I was going to be the barbarian from the plains? Bite somebody?"

She was delighted and more than a little shaken at his suggestion of their having a drink together. The words tumbled out of her mouth before she thought about them. "I thought you'd be just wonderful. And you were."

A peculiar expression crossed his face as he looked down at her. Tess turned her face away, embarrassed. She knew she had been gazing at him with adoration.

"I hope Bunny's feeling better," he said, his voice gruff. He pulled his tie looser. "That kid's always had a nervous stomach. Maybe this'll help teach her that New York isn't the place for her. What she needs is to go to college, settle down."

The elevator doors opened, and they stepped onto the deep, wine-colored carpet of the hallway. "If I get that job," Tess said, swallowing hard, "I won't be back in Omaha for very long. But I meant what I said. I'll try to find a good photographer who'll take Bunny on as an apprentice. I promise."

He seemed to take no note that Tess was about to depart permanently from his life. "I'd still rather she'd go to college," Cal grumbled, unlocking his door and swinging it open.

As soon as the door stood open, Tess realized that something was wrong. The room was dark and silent. It felt empty.

Foreboding pulsed through her. She stared into the shadows, not wanting to think what they meant.

She felt Cal tense beside her. He swore softly and switched on the lights. The room was disordered but deserted. The closet door was open, and Bunny's clothes were not inside. Neither was there any sign of her suitcase.

A note scribbled on hotel stationery lay on the coffee table, held in place by a crystal ashtray.

Tess stood paralyzed by the door. Slowly Cal walked to the table and picked up the note. His face was pale, its muscles rigid. He read the words scrawled in Bunny's looping hand. Then he raised his gaze to meet Tess's.

The look in his eyes frightened her. He had the expression of a man so deeply angered and stunned that he might do anything.

"What is it?" she asked. But she already knew.

"She's gone off to marry Fred Fortcscue. He followed her here," he said. "My God." He sank into a chair, looking as if he'd been hit.

Tess could say nothing. She stood tensed, watching him.

He crumpled the paper and let it fall. "I lost her." He shook his head in disbelief. "I failed her, and I lost her. She's gone."

His words and the look on his face stabbed through her like a blade of ice.

CHAPTER TEN

THEY SAT UP half the night in the hotel room, drinking coffee and making useless phone calls. The police would not look for Bunny because she was not officially a missing person.

Cal sat on the edge of the bed, his collar open and his sleeves rolled up. He hung up the phone and ran his hand through his hair. He had just finished talking to a lawyer.

"She's underage, so a marriage could be annulled," he muttered. "But it's valid until then. And she's only two weeks from legal age. This guy says probably no court would void the marriage if Bunny really wants it. And by the time it did, she'd be old enough to do it over legally. Damn!"

Tess sat on the floor near his feet, her shoes and earrings off. She finished the last of her cold coffee and reread Bunny's hastily scribbled note for the dozenth time:

Dear Uncle Cal—
I love you and Edna, but Freddy and I belong to each other and we have destinys to follow so we're getting married as soon as possible. We thought it all out carefully and decided this is the best way. We won't be going back to Nebraska, it's time to make our break. Go home without me. I'll call you there some time next week. Be happy for me! I really do love you! And I really do appreciate you! I love Edna, too! Tell her I'm

fine and I'll think of you both every day. Fred and I are
artists. We have to do this.

Bunny

Tess rubbed her eyes wearily. Bunny had misspelled the
word *destinies*. Tess hoped it wasn't a bad omen.

Cal massaged his neck, then shook his head. "They
probably went over the border into Vermont. You can get
married there without a waiting period. By this time tomorrow it'll be done. Well, she's got what she wanted. She's
free. If 'free' is what you can call being hooked to Fred
Fortescue for life."

"Cal," Tess said, looking up at him, "you don't know.
Maybe things will work out for them."

He sat with his elbows on his knees, one hand still rubbing the muscles at the back of his neck. "Yeah. Maybe the
sun will rise in the west. Maybe the cow will jump over the
moon."

"I mean," she said earnestly, "she's an extremely talented girl. And this Fred's obviously mad about her. If he's
smart enough to teach college, then he ought to be smart
enough to get along in New York."

He didn't seem to hear her. "I know exactly what she'll
do if I object. She'll get pregnant. That's all she needs. A
baby having a baby." He swore, put his feet up on the
spread and lay back, his hands behind his head on the pillow. He stared at the ceiling.

Tess knelt beside the bed. "I'm sure that girls younger
than Bunny have married men sillier than Fred, but still,
somehow, things came out all right. You did everything for
her you could—"

He swiveled his head to glare at her. "Look who's here.
The advertising woman, whose profession is telling pleasant lies. Don't give me the commercial spiel for blissful
teenage marriage. I don't want to hear it. Switch it off."

Stricken, Tess said nothing. He had every right to be angry. His hair had fallen over his forehead, and she had the urge to smooth it back, but she knew better than to do so. She clenched and unclenched her hand helplessly.

He turned his long body, propping himself up on one elbow. He reached out his other hand and took Tess's chin between his thumb and forefinger. When he spoke, his voice was as harsh as his face. "But don't stop cheering for her, Tess. She's doing her own thing—just like you thought she should—even if it's disastrous. Go ahead and cheer. She'll need it. Because she's not as old as you, or as educated, or as experienced. Or as cold. But go ahead and babble about how it'll work out for her. Just don't do it in front of me."

"I—" Tess began.

"You," he said, leaning closer, his hand tightening around her jaw, "have a job interview in the morning. For the big time. I don't want to keep you from your beauty sleep."

"Cal—" she pleaded, tears stinging her eyes, "I didn't mean for this to happen. I didn't understand about Bunny. I wouldn't have had this happen—"

"Shh," he admonished. "It's happened. But what do you care? You're in New York. You've got what you want."

I don't. I didn't want any of this, she wanted to cry.

"Are those tears I see," he mocked, tilting her face more fully toward his. "Why? I just told you. You have everything you want now. Why cry? I'm the one who's paid for it—and Bunny, of course, will pay too. A kid who's probably just ruined her life."

"I don't want you to think that of me," she said desperately. "Please don't feel—"

"Ah, Tess," he said, holding her fast, his voice more taunting than before. "You do tears so well. They make your eyes shine like brown sherry by candlelight. You care what I think? You care what I feel? If you'd ever done that, you'd have left me alone in the first place, wouldn't you?''

"I don't want you to—"

"Shh," he said, interrupting her. "After all this, you want my good opinion, too? I'm touched. You'll be going your own way now, and I wish you the best."

"No," she said, her voice choked.

"You don't believe me? Then here's a kiss for good luck."

He drew nearer, tilting her face up so that her lips fit against his. The touch of his mouth on hers shook Tess to the center of her soul. Her cool lips trembled against his warm ones. Her whole body trembled.

She had read things in his kisses before, whether anger or desire. This time she sensed a different emotion radiating from his taut body. It was regret, but it was mingled with contempt.

She wanted him to keep kissing her until she tasted forgiveness on his lips and a yearning that matched her own. But he drew back, saying "Good luck. And goodbye."

Her lips felt naked without his. His hand fell away from her face, and she felt more naked still. He put his hands behind his head again and stretched out once more to stare at the ceiling. "Leave, Tess," he said. "There's nothing you can do here. You've done it all. Now I've got to figure a way to tell Edna."

Tess stared at him, stunned with hurt. Then she snatched up her shoes and earrings, rose and strode barefoot toward the door. She turned and looked back at him as he stared impassively at the ceiling.

She started to say again that she was sorry but knew it would do no good. Nothing she could say would matter in the least. Humiliated, she stepped into the hall and closed the door behind her. "Bunny," she said, her teeth clenched, "how could you do this to him? *How?*"

But she knew how. Bunny had made Cal's worst nightmare come true. And Tess, unwittingly, had helped her do it, almost every step of the way.

THE NEXT MORNING Cal was gone when she tried to phone him for news of Bunny. Tess went numbly to her interview with Aggy Chadwick at a small but elegant ad agency just off Madison Avenue. She felt cold and robotlike during the interview, but perhaps a robot was precisely what the Chadwick woman wanted; she offered Tess the job on the spot. Tess smiled a cool, mechanical smile and said, yes, she'd take it. She'd need a week in Nebraska to put her affairs in order.

When she returned to the hotel, she was distressed to find that Cal had checked out, having left only a short note for her at the desk. Standing in the elegant lobby, she tore open the envelope, feeling more numb than before.

> Bunny married in Vermont this A.M. I'm going back to help Edna get through this. I'd say it's been fun, but it hasn't, has it?
>
> Cal

She stood for a moment, staring across the marble lobby to the brass framed doors that led outside.

"Are you all right, miss?" asked the desk clerk. He looked tense, as if he feared she might faint, an untidy crisis unfit for such a fine hotel.

"I'm fine," Tess said, but in truth, everything around her moved as if in slow motion, and the world had become meaningless, no more real than a half-remembered dream.

Somehow she stayed another two days in New York, moving to a less expensive hotel. She lined up a tiny studio apartment in the village that probably cost far too much and was located altogether too far from her job, but it didn't matter. She was simply going through the motions. The important thing, she told herself, was to keep moving, to keep acting like a normal human being.

Then, she was flying back to Nebraska, giving notice to her landlord, packing her few belongings, donating most of her furniture to the Salvation Army. She and Delia had a farewell lunch and a good cry over saying goodbye, but somehow even that didn't seem quite real to Tess. It was as if everything was happening behind a thick wall of glass and she was insulated from it.

"Are you all right?" Delia asked with concern as they parted. "You seem kind of—funny."

"I'm fine," Tess lied. She hadn't told Delia about Bunny's running away. She was too ashamed of her part in it.

Then, magically, she was back in New York, and the atmosphere of the city swirled around her like the pattern in a kaleidoscope gone mad. Manhattan, she quickly decided, contained every dream she had ever hungered after in the secret recesses of her heart. It also harbored most of the nightmares that had ever haunted her most bedeviled sleep.

There were beautiful people in beautiful clothing. The window displays in the stores on Fifth Avenue dazzled her. There were films and theaters and cabarets and bistros and wonderful restaurants. Museums bulged with treasures of every sort. Galleries housed a wealth of art. The whole city hummed with vitality, talent and power. New York was a shrine to all the best that humanity could offer.

There were also crowds and noise and traffic, all in amounts that Tess found staggering. There were people who looked enormously wealthy and those who looked not only penniless but homeless. There were those who looked criminal and some who looked dangerous and some who seemed frankly insane, standing on curbs and shouting terrible things at strangers or even at the sky.

Once Tess saw a man fall down on the sidewalk and lie there. Nobody stopped to help him. They simply stepped over or around him, and frightened, Tess did, too, although she knew she would feel guilty about it for the rest of her life.

She saw a man accidently killed by a car and another man who seemed to be trying to kill himself, darting on foot in and out of the traffic. He was screaming and weeping, and finally the police came and led him away. He haunted Tess's dreams for weeks afterward.

One day, walking on 42nd Street at high noon, she felt a stinging sensation at her neck and realized that her gold chain necklace had been jerked off her throat. After that when she was on the street, she felt constantly on guard, like a small animal that knows it's easy prey. If New York offered the best that humanity was capable of, it also offered the worst.

Her apartment was as cramped as a closet, and she could not comprehend what the man next door did unless his hobby was beating on things with a sledgehammer. All evening and most of the night slamming noises jarred through the walls. On the other side was a woman who aspired to be an opera singer and practiced constantly. Tess, although she could not speak German, soon learned every piercing word of the soprano's part in *Die Zauberflauote*.

What Tess found most unsettling was her job. Aggy Chadwick's agency seemed to move at three times the speed of the ones in Omaha, but Tess wasn't sure it was any more efficient. There seemed to be too many people with too much money at stake for anything to be done quickly or simply. Migraines, ulcers, muscle spasms and anxiety attacks abounded among the staff, and consequently so did tranquilizers and three-martini lunches.

Worst was her list of clients. There was *Tom Cat* magazine, a man's magazine so sexist that Tess could hardly bear to pick it up, let alone sing its praises.

A medium-sized airline wanted to mount a campaign to improve its image. Its reputation suffered because its flights were seldom on time, its handlers perpetually sent luggage to a destination different from the owner's, and the planes themselves had a disturbing tendency to lose power and be forced to land in cornfields or on interstate highways. The day before Tess took over the account, the company had the biggest accident of its history. "Give this campaign all you've got," advised Aggie Chadwick. "I want you to sell it as hard as you can. But, just between friends, if you value your life don't ever get on one of their planes."

Tess's third big account was Ocean D-Lite Tuna. Tess never bought Ocean D-Lite Tuna because the company was infamous for using the sort of nets that trapped dolphins, entangling or drowning them. On more than one occasion they had been investigated for grinding up the dead dolphins for use in their subsidiary product, Kitty-Yum-Yum canned cat food.

Slowly the summer passed. Tess wrote copy for *Tom Cat* magazine, although she wouldn't read it, for AirStreak Airline, although she wouldn't fly it, and for D-Lite Tuna, although she wouldn't eat it. She found herself thinking longingly of a farm in northeast Nebraska and a tall man who liked honesty, peace and quiet.

One hot afternoon at the end of July, she stepped outside the office building, mentally trying to prepare herself to squeeze into the subway crowd. The pavement was so hot it burned through the soles of her shoes. Someone tapped her on the shoulder.

Startled, fearing a mugger, she whirled and looked into a pair of bright hazel eyes—Bunny's.

"Hi!" Bunny grinned. "How're you doing? Is this a great city or what? Don't you *love* it?"

The girl had surprised Tess so much that she felt almost breathless. Except Bunny no longer looked like a girl. She looked like a young woman. She looked, in fact, exactly the way a young New Yorker ought to look: confident, energetic, voguish.

Bunny's hair was lightened to an almost pinkish blond and cut in an avant-garde style. Her clothes were trendy as tomorrow, and she had a camera case slung over her shoulder. She wore a dangling set of earrings made from beads and tiny bones.

"Bunny—how are you?" Tess asked, although what she wondered was how Cal was. She knew she should be angry at Bunny, but she was so glad to see a familiar face that anger, for the moment, evaporated.

"I'm *great*," Bunny said. "I've got a day job working for a children's photographer—kid's portraits and stuff—very upscale. Nights I do my own thing. I did a series of pictures on bag ladies, and *Earthworks* magazine bought one—and gave me an assignment, besides. On wild animal life in the city. I got a rat shot last night you wouldn't believe."

Bunny looked so vibrant, so full of life and excitement that Tess felt tired and dowdy beside her. "Bunny, that's wonderful. How's Fred?"

"Fred's *great*," Bunny said with enthusiasm. "He hasn't found any acting jobs yet, but he's making jewelry." She shook her head so that the bead and bone earrings rattled. "See? Like them?"

"They're very...interesting," Tess said vaguely, her heart sinking. Cal was right. Fred wasn't working. Bunny, barely eighteen, must be supporting them both.

"These earrings are made of chicken ribs mostly," Bunny said, shaking her head again. "And everybody's buying them. He does bracelets and necklaces, too. He can't make them fast enough. He's thinking about giving up acting altogether. I mean, jewelry making's an art, too. In one of the really good boutiques, his necklaces sell for four hundred dollars."

Tess blinked in surprise and stared at the dangling bones and beads. Of course, she thought, slightly dizzy, this is New York, and anything could happen. Perfectly sane people might suddenly decide that it was fashionable to wear chicken bones for jewelry.

Although Tess was glad for Fred's success, even relieved by it, she wasn't interested in dwelling on it. "Your uncle," she said hesitantly, "have you been in touch?"

"Oh, sure," Bunny said. "He's fine. Listen, do you want to do lunch sometime?"

"Of course," Tess replied. "But how is he? How's he reacting to—you know—your getting married? Is he angry at Fred? How's Edna?"

Bunny shrugged, taking out her camera. "He's okay. He's adjusting. He'll learn to accept Fred. Edna's great—she always has been. We're going out there for Christmas. How's your job?"

Tess gritted her teeth. Bunny certainly wasted no energy on details. "The job's fine," she lied. "But your uncle...he was deeply disturbed when you ran off—"

Bunny trained her camera on a bedraggled pigeon that was peering into a battered trash can in an alley. "He's getting over it," she said without concern. "He's just got to learn I'm not the same person as my mother, that's all. I can take care of myself. Believe me." She clicked the camera shutter once, then twice.

Bunny lowered the camera and dug into the depths of a fashionably shapeless black purse. "Here—" she said, handing Tess a slip of paper. "My phone number. Call me. We'll have lunch. Who knows? Your agency may have work for me. It handles the Wilmer Toy company, doesn't it?

Well, I'm learning to do just a heck of a job photographing kids—who knows—maybe you can use me.''

She gave Tess a dazzling smile and was gone, vanishing into the crowd, one New Yorker among hundreds of others.

She's thriving on this, Tess thought. *Blooming and thriving. She was right all along. She belongs here.*

Tess met Bunny three more times. Always any anger she felt for the girl was overwhelmed by wonder at how well she seemed to be doing in New York.

They had lunch once. Once she went shopping with Bunny for antique beads, and once she went to Bunny and Fred's apartment for supper. Fred, she discovered, was tall, blond, handsome and not particularly brilliant. But he obviously adored Bunny, believed in her and would do anything she wished to make her happy. Although he was older and more educated, Bunny was clearly the partner in charge. They both seemed to like it that way.

Tess should have been happy that Bunny had adjusted so perfectly to life in New York. It meant she herself didn't have to feel guilty for being part of the forces that had brought Bunny here.

The more she saw of Bunny, in fact, the more she realized that Bunny always had and always would be the mistress of her own fate. The girl had been born convinced of her own importance and determined to go her own way. She was bold and could be unscrupulous if she chose. When she wanted something, heaven help whoever tried to keep her from it. She was as vital as a force of nature.

Somehow, though, Bunny depressed Tess. It was as if Bunny, so pleased with everything in life, made Tess even more dissatisfied with her own. Above all, she made Tess remember Cal, and remembering hurt like the stab of a knife. She had once thought she and Bunny shared the same dreams. Now she realized that every woman's dream was different, and she was no closer to knowing hers than she had been back in Omaha.

Still, in the middle of August, she made a date to meet Bunny on a Saturday afternoon to go to an exhibit of nineteenth century photographs. As usual, she was thinking about Cal. For the thousandth time she wondered if she should contact him and tell him how well Bunny seemed. For the thousandth time she realized she didn't have the courage to try. She was just fastening her gold earrings when her phone rang.

She answered it and was at first surprised, then disturbed, to hear the voice of her oldest brother, Sarton. It was the first she'd heard from any of her family since she'd written them that she was leaving for New York.

"Dad's sick," Sarton said, abrupt as ever. "He had a heart attack. He wants to see you. I think you'd better come."

Tess's heart leaped in fright and a wild tumble of emotions coursed through her. Her father couldn't be sick. Her father was so strong and stubborn and tough that he would live forever, and nothing could even hurt him, let alone kill him.

"Heart attack? How bad? Where is he?"

"Bad. In the hospital in Omaha. St. Joseph's. Look, can you come or not?"

She set her jaw, trying to steady herself. Her emotions about her father were deep and complicated. Sarton's curtness didn't improve matters, but she supposed Sarton couldn't help that. He'd always been close-mouthed, and the telephone was not an instrument he liked. She couldn't expect him to change now, even if their father was ill enough to call for her.

Ill enough to call for me, she thought, feeling almost sick herself. He must be seriously stricken if he had put aside his pride and asked for her. But if he had asked for her, she thought with a bound of hope, perhaps he still loved her.

And, shaken, Tess knew at that moment that she still loved him. She had tried to pretend she didn't, she had told herself she didn't, she had acted as if she didn't, she had even pretended she no longer loved the land, but it was all a lie to keep herself from being hurt more deeply than she had been. He was her father, and she loved him.

"I'll be there as soon as I can," Tess told Sarton. "Tell him I'm coming."

She called Bunny to cancel their outing, then phoned Aggy Chadwick to say she'd be gone from work for a while. Aggy wasn't pleased. "Tess," she said icily, "you're behind on that AirStreak account. You haven't turned in one convincing line of copy. And the absolute deadline is next week."

"Mrs. Chadwick, it's hard to be enthusiastic about an airline that's nicknamed 'AirSick.' They had a DC10 crash land on a golf course in New Jersey yesterday. It's a miracle nobody was killed."

"You don't have to believe in them. Just sell them," Aggy Chadwick snapped. "It's your *job*."

I was better off when I had to make the chickens dress in high heels and the chimpanzee cook spaghetti, Tess thought darkly. "I'll write it on the plane," she promised. She hung up, then dialed for reservations to Omaha.

Ironically, the first flight she could get was on AirStreak Airlines. They lost her luggage, had engine trouble and arrived in Omaha five hours behind schedule. She did not, of course, write one line of convincing copy.

HER BROTHERS had little to say to her, even though it had been a long time since she had met them face to face. They were not men comfortable with expressing emotion. But she could tell they were troubled, and she thought they were glad that she'd arrived.

Sarton escorted her almost wordlessly to their father's room, and Tess felt her heart hammering in apprehension.

How sick was her father? she wondered. What would he say to her? And she to him? Was it a terrible mistake coming here? Would they merely discover once again that they had nothing in common and could never please each other?

She and Sarton came to a door, and she knew by some strange instinct it was *the door*. "He'd like to see you alone," Sarton said, his voice gruff.

Tess put her hand on the knob. She looked up at her brother. He was a big man, rugged-looking with dark eyes and curling auburn hair. "Sarton, you know I never meant to hurt anybody when I went off. All I wanted was—"

"I understand," Sarton said. "We all understand." He turned and left her there, her hand on the knob.

Had he understood? she wondered, squaring her shoulders. She had never known what her brothers thought or felt. They had been one reason it hadn't been difficult to leave home. It was as if emotion was a weakness not to be admitted, affection a frailty not to be displayed. And her father—she didn't know what to think about her father. Suddenly she wished she was back in the madness of New York, where her heart was safe from these uncommunicative men.

She turned the knob and went inside the hospital room.

Her father lay on the bed, his head raised by the pillow. He was hooked to some sort of machine that monitored his heartbeat. When he saw her, she thought that the blip on the screen speeded up and bounced more erratically, and that frightened her. So did his pallor, although otherwise he looked as big and strong as ever.

The two of them looked at each other a long moment.

"Daddy?" she said, at last, because she didn't know what else to say. "Are you all right?"

He was not a man who smiled often, and he did not smile now. He looked at her but did not speak.

She walked numbly to his side. Then, because it seemed right to do so, she bent and kissed his cheek, and she laid her face against his shoulder. He made no movement and still said nothing.

Then she felt his hand touch her hair almost hesitantly. Almost immediately he drew his hand away. She raised her face and looked into his eyes. His face was taut, unhappy.

"I missed you, Tess," he said at last, his voice low. "I'm sorry I drove you off."

The words obviously cost him a great deal. He looked away from her. Tess took his hand, blinking back tears.

She tried to say she was sorry, too, but could not.

He squeezed her hand awkwardly before letting it go. He had never been the sort for emotional displays. He glanced at her, then away again. He stared toward the window. "Don't try to say anything. It's me that has to apologize. Don't cry." Tess tried to choke back the tears but couldn't. She reached for his hand again.

He let her take it. "All right," he said wearily. "Cry. I could never keep your mother from crying when she had a mind to. You were like her, you know. The boys took after me. But you, you were just like her."

Tess scrubbed the tears away with the back of her hand. She bit her lip to keep it from trembling. She could tell that her father had thought a long time about what he wanted to say, and her crying would only make it harder for him.

He kept gazing at the window, but he let her hold his hand. "Your mother loved that farm. She went back to work so we could keep it. I didn't want her to do it, but she did. And then she died. I blamed myself. I hadn't been able to provide."

Tess bit her lip harder and watched her father's face. It was paler than before and almost expressionless, but his chin trembled slightly.

"You mean," Tess asked, her voice strained, "you thought if you'd made more money, she wouldn't have had to go to work? She wouldn't have died?"

"I didn't think it, I knew it," he said bitterly. "That piece of land was sucking the blood out us, and she died to save it. So I sold the damned place, for once and all."

"But Daddy, we all loved the farm," Tess said, her voice shaking. "You did, too."

"I couldn't keep it," he said, shaking his head. For the first time he looked visibly upset, so she smoothed his gray hair back from his forehead.

"Listen, Tess," he said, his voice rasping, "you have to understand. Even when you were little, I wasn't good at showing my feelings. I had them, but I didn't show them. That was your mother's job. She knew what they were. I felt crazy after she died. You were so much like her, I didn't want you getting fancy ideas and going away. She'd been to college, you know. That's why she could work in the law office. I tried to keep part of her by keeping you. But I—I tried too hard. I drove you off." He was silent a moment. "It was like losing her a second time. And I was too proud to say I was wrong. Until now. Looking Death in the eye teaches a man how little pride's worth. She'd have hated what I did to you. Lord knows she'd have hated it. I've got to put it right."

He looked bone weary, so tired that Tess was frightened. She rang for the nurse.

"Hear me out," her father said. "I hung on to you so tight, I forced you to break away. I'm sorry. I'm proud of you. I'm very, very proud of you. And proud that you came home again."

Once more Tess fought to keep the tears from brimming in her eyes. He had never before said he loved her or that he was sorry. And never, since her mother had died, could she remember him saying he was proud of her.

"I love you, too," she said, squeezing his hand. For the first time, he smiled. She bent and kissed his cheek again.

Then the nurse came and made her go away.

THREE DAYS LATER, the doctors cautiously said that they thought her father was out of danger. Tess planned to go back to New York on Sunday night, but first she knew she should talk to Cal and Edna. She wanted them to know that she had seen Bunny and that the girl seemed happy and safe and well.

When she tried to call, however, the operator told her the number had been changed and was now unlisted.

"I think that man just hates phones," Delia said. Tess was staying at Delia's house, and the two of them met near the hospital for lunch almost every day.

"Phone calls probably drove him crazy after that television show," Tess murmured, bending the straw in her drink. She and Delia sat in the booth of a small restaurant with brick walls and a multitude of potted ferns.

"Women calling up to propose probably," Delia said with a rueful laugh. "We got a dozen calls at the agency from women chasing after him. I never thought it'd be a burden to be good-looking. But it must be. Does anybody ever get past the poor man's looks? No wonder he lives the quiet life."

Delia's words gave her a pang. "I wish I could get in touch with them. I guess I could write," she said wistfully.

Delia studied her friend and sighed. She reached into her purse and took out her car keys. "Don't write," she said, and taking Tess's hand, she dropped the keys in it. "Go see him. You need to. I can tell." She closed Tess's fingers around the keys.

"Take your car again? Delia, I couldn't," Tess said, aghast. "Besides, I shouldn't leave my father and brothers. I probably won't get home again till Christmas."

Delia squeezed Tess's hand more tightly shut around the keys. "You can miss one afternoon with your father. As for your brothers, well, excuse me, but they don't strike me as sentimental types."

Delia made such a wry face that Tess almost smiled. Her brothers were polite in their way, but they were almost as detached as they had been years ago, when they'd considered her a grade-school pest, beneath their dignity to notice. But her father, at least, did not seem embarrassed by how much emotion he had shown her. He still didn't lavish affection on Tess, but for the first time she could remember since she was a child, he let it shine, unashamed, out of his eyes.

Tess fingered the keys, looking at them. "You won't have a way home. I can't make it to Lawler and back by five o'clock."

"You don't have to," Delia said with great self-satisfaction. "I have a date. With Henderson Bailey."

"Henderson Bailey?" Tess practically cried. "*The* Henderson Bailey? The one you were so madly in love with in junior college?"

"The very one. He moved back from St. Louis," Delia said. She heaped her hair on top of her head and assumed a pose of mock sexiness. "And he remembered yours truly. So why don't you just run along for the evening? Delia has dealings, darlin'."

Delia let her hair fall back into place, frowning slightly. "Didn't you apply for a job up that way? At that college? Up near the Buchanon man? What happened?"

"Nothing," Tess replied. "They hired somebody else. They said they'd keep me in mind."

Delia gave her a thoughtful look. "And what if they'd said yes? Would you have gone up there to work, instead of to New York?"

Tess looked away. It was a question she couldn't answer. "I don't know," she said.

"Tess, did you hear yourself a minute ago?" Delia asked. "What you said?"

She shook her head. "No."

"You called this 'home'." Delia paused. "What did you mean by that? Frontier County? Omaha? Nebraska? Is your home in Nebraska? Have you decided that it is?"

Tess took a deep breath. "I don't know that, either," she said. But she knew. Nebraska was her home. It always had been. It always would be.

TESS'S HEART beat erratically as she approached the little town of Lawler. The hills and fields outside town blazed with the last sumptuous green of summer, the sky was a vast sweep of blue and white, and the sun poured down its golden brilliance.

The town dozed in the afternoon sun. With college out for the summer, no students strolled the sidewalks, and few townsmen braved the heat. The wide brick streets were almost empty. A few children played on a lawn, jumping in and out of the shower of a sprinkler. In one yard a large white dog slept blissfully on his back in the sun, all four paws in the air.

How could such a drowsy place look and feel so good, Tess wondered uneasily. After the cramped concrete mazes of Manhattan, the quiet streets stretched before her like a leaf-shaded path to heaven.

That was silly, Tess told herself. There was nothing in this corner of the state for her, no home, no work, no friends, no purpose.

There's nothing at all for me here, she thought, *except the feeling that I belong.*

She shook her head to clear it. She knew she would come back to the Midwest, though not to this precise part. She had known she'd come back from the first day she'd lived in New York. It was the idea of the city she had loved, not its reality. Its pace was foreign, hectic and hazardous to her. Unlike Bunny, she could never love it. And unlike Bunny, she could never belong there.

She left Lawler and turned down the highway that led to Cal's. Her heart and pulses were doing unpleasantly fast-paced things again, and she realized she was frightened to confront him. She was even a bit afraid to confront Edna.

The one good thing that had come from the whole muddle, she told herself, was that advance sales for the calendar were phenomenal; Delia had said so. Delia had also said that Cal's appearance on The Morty Jessen Show had had an impact. The Homestead Heritage Foundation had decided to do exactly what he'd recommended, earmark a large part of the funds for educational programs to help beleaguered farmers, to teach them to adjust their crops to a changing economy. Would Cal be pleased by that? Or would he greet the news with coldness? Would he even talk to her?

When she approached the pasture nearest the house, she saw a tall man with dark hair taking the rope from the neck of a gawky palomino colt. He wore blue jeans, a blue work shirt with rolled up sleeves, and a black cowboy hat pushed far back on his head.

Cal, she thought, and it seemed as if every cell of her body sang out his name.

Without thinking, she pulled to the side of the road and parked the car. She got out, closing the door, oblivious of the tall weeds that tickled her legs and brushed the hem of her skirt. Quickly she stepped through the grasses, drew her skirt out of the way and slipped between the strands of barbed wire that separated the pasture from the road.

Her dress, a dusky pale pink with a halter top, was not the sort of thing to wear to cross a pasture, and neither were the matching shoes, but Tess didn't care. One of the fence barbs scratched her arm, but she barely noticed.

Cal had straightened and stood, the rope coiled in his hand, watching her come. She could not see his expression, for his hat shaded his face, but every line of his body looked tensed with wariness.

The palomino colt tossed its head in her direction, nickered nervously, switched its broomlike tail and skittered off at a trot to join its mother, grazing near the fence on the pasture's far side.

Cal turned from her, giving her a sidelong glance, then headed for the shade of a line of large lilac bushes that formed a windbreak between the pasture and the house.

He was going to ignore her, she thought in panic, not even acknowledge her presence. She wanted to cry out for him to stop, but the words stuck in her throat. She began to run.

He reached the cool sanctuary of the lilac bushes and turned, looking at her again. She had nearly caught up with him, and wanted to talk to him so badly that she could not stop herself from running toward him, even though the high-heeled shoes made her gait awkward.

He took off the broad-rimmed black hat and wiped his forehead with the back of his hand. Tess was close enough to see that he was so deeply tanned that his hazel eyes looked golden. He stared at her and let the hat drop to the ground.

"Please—" she said breathlessly. "Please—?"

Then she stumbled, and he stepped forward, catching her. For a moment she rested against the warm, hard wall of his chest, felt the shelter of his strong arms. The scent of him filled her nostrils, hay and grass and horsehair and clean summer sweat.

Shaken, she stared up at him. He looked, as usual, handsomer than any man she had ever seen, but that was not what mattered. What mattered was that he was Cal.

As soon as she was steady on her feet again, he drew back from her. He kept his hands on her upper arms, but almost as if he were holding her, not to him, but away from him.

"Please," she said, finding it hard to get her breath. "Don't walk away from me. Just listen. For a moment."

His face was stern, unyielding. "I'm not walking away. What are you doing? You'll get sunstroke running like that. Are you crazy? Look at yourself."

She looked down. Her skirt was studded with cockleburrs, her stockings were ruined, her skimpy shoes dusty and stained with grass.

"You're bleeding, too," he said with disgust. He turned her around, almost roughly, and began dabbing at her scratched arm with a clean bandanna.

"Bunny's fine," she almost panted, trying to look over her shoulder at him. "I've seen her. Honestly, Cal, she's taken to New York as if she was born for it. She seems wonderfully happy. And both she and Fred are working."

"I know that." He turned her back to face him again, his hands still on her arms. "Is that all you came to tell me?"

She took in her breath sharply. The look on his face was so intent it filled her with apprehension, but his touch tingled through her body. His hands against her flesh made her quake within. "Yes," she said at last. "I thought I should tell you and Edna. That I've actually seen her. That she's happy."

He shook his head. He stared down at her and said nothing. He released her. She took a step backward to escape the magnetism of his nearness. He watched her, his eyes even more intent than before. "I know she's happy," he said at last. "I've seen her myself. You didn't have to come clear up here to tell me that."

Tess blinked in surprise. "You've seen her? When?"

He shrugged, a restless movement. "I went last week. To see if she needed anything. She doesn't. She's got what she needs. You were right. I was wrong. She needed her freedom. She needed New York. Maybe she even needs that idiot, Fred. How's your father?"

"What?" She looked at him in confusion. "How do you know about that?"

"I wanted to see you in New York," he said. He jammed his thumbs into his back pockets. He looked up at the sky as if checking for weather signs. "Bunny said you'd come back to Omaha because your father was sick. How is he?"

He dropped his gaze from the sky and stared off across the meadow, still not looking at her. She wondered why he looked so impassive, yet unhappy at the same time.

"My father's going to be fine, they think."

He nodded to indicate that the news was good. "I take it you made up with him?"

"Yes," she said. "You were right, too. He didn't do what he did out of meanness. In his way, he did it out of love. I understand better now. And he understands that I did what I had to do, too."

The line of his mouth grew more rigid. His gaze met hers at last, jolting her down to her heels. "And what about you?" he asked, his tone harsh. "Are you like Bunny? Are you finally where you need to be? Doing what you want to do?"

For a long moment they simply looked at each other. The wind moved over the grasses, and somewhere a lark sang. Tess swallowed hard. "No."

He seemed to tense slightly but said nothing. He stood, as if waiting for her to explain. The sky behind him was blue and vibrant. Another lark called to the first.

"New York isn't where I need to be. And advertising isn't what I need to do. I thought maybe I'd come—" she took another deep breath "—come home. Try a teaching job."

He nodded again. He passed the back of his hand over his mouth. "Any place special?" he asked, as if it didn't concern him.

"No," she answered. She felt the wind in her hair, tousling it. "Wherever they'll have me, I guess."

He stared at the sky again. "There's a college here. Would you consider that?"

A meadowlark soared up from a patch of Queen Anne's lace, and Tess's heart seemed to soar with it. She didn't know why he asked, and she didn't dare to hope. If she didn't know better, she would think he was almost shy with her.

"I applied. They turned me down." She stood a bit straighter because she felt so self-conscious with him. The wind stirred the fullness of her skirt, and she let its fluttering folds hide her hands.

He continued to study the sky as if it were a book in which he could read secrets. "So I heard."

"You heard?" She was puzzled.

"I know people at the college. There's another opening now, you know. Since Fred left. They haven't filled it yet. You could apply for that."

She raised her shoulders questioningly. "I didn't know. But I didn't think . . . you'd want me around."

He lowered his gaze to hers again. Tess's heart bolted like one of his little colts. A muscle worked in his jaw. "I want you around," he said. "I've wanted you around since the first time I saw you."

His words seemed to make the sky go so blue it dazzled Tess. The blueness almost wheeled around Cal's figure, making her dizzy and confused. Had he said he wanted her? That he'd always wanted her? Had he really said that?

She could not speak. She could only stare up at him. His face was bronze against the blue of the sky, his hair glistening black.

The muscles in his jaw showed his emotions were as intense as her own. "I didn't want you to go to New York. I couldn't believe you were meant to be there. That's why I wanted to see you when I was there. To find out if you'd had your fill of it. That and to tell you I was wrong to blame you for Bunny. Nobody could have stopped her. I know she's found her place. But you—I thought you were different. That you'd be ready to come home."

Suddenly she felt shaky all over, as if the day were cold instead of hot. "Yes," she said. "I'm ready."

He took a step closer to her. He looked down at her for a long moment, then swept her into his arms and kissed her with a passion that made her feel half-faint. She put her arms around his neck and pressed closer to him.

"I hated believing you belonged anywhere except with me," he said and crushed her more tightly to him. "I couldn't get you out of my head. I wanted you the way a man wants air or food or sleep—something he has to have to live."

"Oh, Cal," she said against his shoulder, "you were right—if I'd really wanted to go to New York, I'd have gone long ago. New York's Bunny's place. It's Fred's place. It's a lot of people's place. But it isn't mine. My home is here."

"Here," he said, against her hair.

She felt more trembly than before. She raised her face to his and nodded.

The meadowlark sang again. "Are you sure you can be happy here?" he asked, touching her cheek. "A life like this?"

She nodded again, tears in her eyes. "Cal—for years I fought what the land meant to me. I fought the fact that I didn't always like advertising all that much. And then I fought the idea of coming home from New York—I thought I'd be a failure. Then I realized I'd be a failure if I didn't. Because I'd be turning my back on everything I loved."

He took her face between his hands. "Your going to New York wasn't a mistake. It had to happen. So you could find out where you belong. And I hope it's here, because I love you."

She smiled up into his eyes. She didn't know if it was the larks singing or her heart.

"I love you," she said.

"Then come home," he said. His mouth closed over hers, and he took her there.

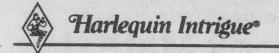

Harlequin Intrigue®

A SPAULDING & DARIEN MYSTERY
by Robin Francis

An engaging pair of amateur sleuths—Jenny Spaulding and Peter Darien—were introduced to Harlequin Intrigue readers in #147, BUTTON, BUTTON (Oct. 1990). Jenny and Peter will return for further spine-chilling romantic adventures in April 1991 in #159, DOUBLE DARE in which they solve their next puzzling mystery. Two other books featuring Jenny and Peter will follow in the A SPAULDING AND DARIEN MYSTERY series.